Sexually Satisfied

Sexually Satisfied

MELISSA
RANDALL

APHRODISIA

KENSINGTON BOOKS
http://www.kensingtonbooks.com

APHRODISIA are published by

Kensington Publishing Corp.
850 Third Avenue
New York, NY 10022

All Kensington Titles, Imprints, and Distributed Lines are available at special quantity discounts for bulk purchases for sales promotions, premiums, fund-raising, and educational or institutional use.

Special book excerpts or customized printings can also be created to fit specific needs. For details, write or phone the office of the Kensington special sales manager: Kensington Publishing Corp., 850 Third Avenue, New York, NY 10022, attn: Special Sales Department, Phone: 1-800-221-2647.

ISBN-13: 978-0-7582-1589-5
ISBN-10: 0-7582-1589-4

First Kensington Trade Paperback Printing: May 2007

10 9 8 7 6 5 4 3 2 1

Printed in the United States of America

1

"Thank you all for coming," said the casting director, clutching his binder to chest. "You were all terrific, and we'll be in touch soon." He gave the six-foot blonde with the huge fake boobs a wide grin, which she returned with a flick of her long bleached hair. *If this bimbo can convince the balding old fart that she finds him absolutely devastating, then she's an Oscar-caliber actress who deserves the job,* I thought caustically.

I sighed, picked up my tote bag and trudged to the door with the other rejects. Another bomb of an audition. I couldn't even get hired for a tampon commercial. It had been two . . . no, three months since my last job. If I didn't land a role soon, I'd have to go back to the grind of office temping.

As soon as I opened the door and stepped outside, the heat hit me like a blast furnace. I immediately felt sweat beading on my upper lip and trickling between my breasts. Oh, the joy of New York City in August. And now I had to take the subway, the stickiest, stinkiest sauna in the world.

I staggered up to my third-floor apartment, pushed my way in and kicked off my shoes. "Apartment" was a bit of an exaggeration. The ad had described it as a "charming, cozy studio" but "tiny rat hole" was really more accurate. I turned the ancient air conditioner to high; it immediately coughed, sputtered and died. "Goddamnit!" I shouted. I hauled out the floor fan, feeling tears of frustration pricking at my eyes.

Five minutes later I was sitting half naked in front of the fan, sipping iced tea. I tried to remind myself of all the good things in my life. My boyfriend of three months, Steve, was the sweetest guy I'd ever met—and extremely cute in the bargain. I was beginning to wonder if he was The One. Anita, my best friend since sixth grade, was supportive and fun and loyal. Even on a sweltering summer day, New York was infinitely preferable to boring Hanover, New Hampshire. And I'd had some success with my acting career; if I could just hold on until the big break came . . .

My cell phone rang, and before I even flipped it open, my telephonic telepathy set in. I just knew it was Steve. We'd talked about getting together tonight, and now I really needed his company.

"Hey, Gillian," he said. "Have you melted yet in this heat?"

"No, but I wish I could. I had a thoroughly shitty day." I proceeded to moan and groan and complain, knowing Steve would be sympathetic. He'd been through enough lousy auditions before landing the plum role of Winston on the long-running soap *Nights of Passion*.

I finally ran out of complaints. "So, what would you like to do tonight?"

Steve was strangely silent. Usually he was an expert at pulling me out of a bad mood.

"Is something wrong, Steve?"

He hesitated. "No. . . . Well, yes. I don't know how to say this, Gillian. . . . I planned to get together with you tonight to discuss it. But I think it's better to do it over the phone."

I never understood the phrase "my heart sank" until that moment. "You want to break up with me," I said woodenly.

He heaved a long sigh. "I'm sorry, really I am. I like you so much, Gillian, and we had some great times together. But I don't think we're compatible."

My throat tightened. "I don't understand. We're interested in the same things, we're in the same business, we enjoy doing the same things—"

"It's not that. I just think we're not compatible . . . sexually. In bed. It's never been very good for either of us."

I was stunned. True, Steve and I didn't have the best sex life, but, god, I had tried to spice things up. He had never seemed interested in trying anything new. It was the same routine every time.

"Look, Steve, I understand what you're saying, but we could work on it—"

"No . . . Gillian, I'm really sorry. The truth is that I've met someone else."

My shock deepened. I couldn't speak. I just sat there as Steve rambled on, apologizing, swearing it wasn't my fault. . . .

I finally interrupted him. "Okay, Steve, good luck." I hung up abruptly and burst into tears.

Once the worst had subsided, I called Anita's cell. Voice mail, damnit. "Hi, Anita, please call me back as soon as you can. . . . Steve just broke up with me." I hiccupped. "It came out of the blue. I'm feeling lousy right now. . . . Thanks."

I washed my face with cold water, praying Anita would call back soon. *I hope she's not having one of her party-hearty club nights*, I thought. When Anita was in that mood, she made Samantha from *Sex and the City* look like a shrinking violet. But Anita was so honest and grounded, the only person I could really talk to about deep emotional stuff. We'd met when we were both twelve and dreaming of fame and fortune in New

York. A few months after high school graduation, we moved together to the city. My success had been modest, but Anita's modeling career had taken off. She hadn't reached single-moniker supermodel status, but she was well on her way.

My cell rang, and I snatched it up. "Anita?"

"Gillian, are you okay? I got your message. . . . God, I'm so sorry. What happened?"

"I don't know. He just said we weren't compatible in bed. Then he said he'd met 'someone else.' That was it. The end."

"Well, it's his loss." Anita was indignant. "I'll bet this 'someone else' won't last more than a few weeks."

"Doesn't matter." I sighed. "It's true that our sex life was pretty mediocre. Not horrible, just not all that good. I had to fake it several times."

"Girl, you should never have to fake it! Find some guy who knows what the hell he's doing. Why don't we hit some clubs this weekend?"

"Sorry, I can't. I'm spending this weekend in Easthampton with Aunt Mary. Steve was supposed to come, too. I guess that's why he broke up with me tonight—he couldn't bear the thought of an entire weekend with me."

She snorted. "Screw Steve. There are some great clubs out in the Hamptons. . . ."

"Oh, Anita, I'm not up for that yet. I'll just spend a quiet weekend with Aunt Mary. I need to get out of this inferno of a city for a few days and relax."

"Okay, but call me anytime if you want to talk."

"Thanks, Anita, you really are the best. I feel a little better already. Let's get together for coffee on Monday."

The train ride to Easthampton seemed endless. I sniveled most of the way. I felt like the world's ultimate loser—I'd win a reality show based on that concept with no effort at all. I was a mediocre actress who could barely make a living in TV commercials. And apparently I was lousy in bed—couldn't even keep Steve's interest for more than three months.

Aunt Mary met me at the station, and just the sight of her silver hair, bright blue eyes and broad smile was enough to cheer me up. I had told her on the phone that Steve and I had broken up; she was tactful enough not to press for details. Aunt Mary and I had always enjoyed a close relationship; she was more like a much older sister than an aunt. She had retired from acting a few years earlier and had always been my mentor and most enthusiastic cheerleader. Mary had never been a hugely successful actress, but she had been well known in New York as a talented and hard-working professional.

I was sprawled on a chaise longue with her cat, Jasmine, purring on my lap when she came out to the patio with two glasses of iced tea. "Gillian, Jackie and Ken Williams are coming over for cocktails. Ken is bringing his golf partner, some guy named David. Sorry . . . I know you're not in a sociable mood."

Damn! Jackie and Ken Williams were the most boring people on the planet. But they had always been good neighbors to Mary, and she was careful to keep their relationship cordial.

I smiled briefly at Mary. "No problem. Company might be a good distraction for me. I feel pretty skanky; I think I'll have a shower and change." I dumped Jasmine to the ground, ignoring her yowl of annoyance.

I felt almost human again after taking a long, hot shower and changing into a pale blue sundress. I looked at myself critically in a full-length mirror. God, I really had to drop ten pounds . . . maybe fifteen. But my skin looked good, tanned to a honey shade, and the strong sun had brought out golden highlights in my wavy brown hair. Perhaps one day, after I got over the humiliation of Steve dumping me, another man might find me attractive and even enjoy me in bed.

The guests had arrived by the time I stepped out to the patio.

Mary made the introductions. "Gillian, you remember Jackie and Ken . . . and this is their friend David Wentworth."

"Hi, Gillian." He smiled and reached out a hand. I gave it a limp shake, trying hard not to gawk. He wasn't conventionally handsome, but he was striking. Somewhere in his early forties. About six feet tall, with the lean, hard physique of a marine—this man had discipline. Light brown hair just starting to go gray. Full lips, ordinary nose. His eyes were his most stunning feature—glacial blue and penetrating. I felt mesmerized. *Powerful* was the word he brought to mind.

I had a sudden attack of shyness. I dropped my eyes from his face and found myself staring at his crotch. I burned with my easily aroused blush as I looked away, praying he hadn't noticed.

The four of us exchanged the usual pleasantries. I sat on the wicker sofa to alleviate the weak feeling in my knees. David handed me a glass of white wine and sat next to me. Mary, Jackie, and Ken huddled on the other side of the patio, complaining about the hideous new McMansion under construction down the street.

"I understand you're an actress, Gillian." David's voice made me think of brandy—smooth and mellow but potent.

"Yes." Why did my voice sound so squeaky? I cleared my throat. "Although, struggling actress is more accurate. I've performed in a few off-Broadway plays, starred in a couple of commercials . . . nothing really major. And nothing at all recently."

"It's a very tough and frustrating business. But I'm sure you'll make it. You're very pretty and obviously very bright."

It was a superficial and conventional compliment, but it seemed authentic to me when he unleashed his brilliant smile. Perfect teeth, of course.

"Thanks." My voice had spiraled into Minnie Mouse range again. His thigh seemed much too close to mine; I was sure I could feel his body heat through the thin cotton of my dress. "So what do you do?"

"Real estate. My parents owned a firm in Denver, so I grew up in the business. I came to New York for college, decided to stay after graduation and work in the industry here. It took a while, but eventually I started my own company."

"Impressive."

"Well, it took a lot of work. I have to admit I'm a bit of a workaholic . . . but I also take playtime very seriously." His eyes locked onto mine, and my mouth went dry.

At that point Mary, Jackie, and Ken joined the conversation, which promptly turned dull—the weather, golf, politics . . . It was hard not to squirm like a fidgety five-year-old. I was still hugely aware of David sitting so close to me, frequently catching my eyes with his and sending me small, secret smiles. The pheromones were flying.

Finally Jackie and Ken rose to say their good-byes; David stood as well. I felt a wave of disappointment. How could this amazing man disappear from my life so quickly?

David saved the day. "I'm driving back to New York tonight. I'm parked at the end of Jackie and Ken's driveway." He turned his intense gaze on me. "Gillian, would you walk me to my car?"

"Sure, I'd love to." Damnit—squeaky voice again, plus I sounded way too eager. "I'll be back in a little while, Mary."

Mary raised one eyebrow and gave us a brief, enigmatic smile. "Sure, that's fine. Dinner can wait a little bit longer."

Jackie and Ken decided to walk the beach back to their house, thank God. I couldn't have endured their incessant chatter bursting the bubble of attraction that surrounded me and David. We walked slowly down Mary's driveway and even more slowly down the road to Jackie and Ken's driveway and his car. A midnight-blue BMW convertible.

"Nice car." *Great, I sound as inane as Jackie and Ken.*

"Glad you like it. We should go for a drive sometime."

"I'd love to." My confidence was rising; this amazing guy really seemed to like me.

"I enjoyed meeting you, Gillian. I'm just sorry I have to leave so soon."

"Business in the city?"

"Yeah, I have to prepare for an early breakfast meeting on Monday. But I'd love to take you out for dinner sometime. Could I have your number?"

I rattled it off as he wrote it down—with a gold pen in a leather-covered notebook. Apparently his real-estate business was doing pretty well.

"Great, I'll call you soon." He tucked the pen and notebook into his jacket pocket. Then he reached out and touched my hair . . . skimmed his fingers along the curve of my cheek. I thought I'd swoon.

"You're such a pretty little thing," he whispered. "I wish I could take you home with me." Then he was leaning down, pressing his warm, full lips against mine. The kiss was gentle but firm, practiced but somehow surprising. I wrapped my arms around his neck, caressed the taut muscles of his back and his chest. He smelled wonderful—a spicy-sweet scent I couldn't quite identify.

He kissed me harder, more urgently. I felt lost. . . .

I'm kissing a stranger in the middle of the street! I dropped my arms and pulled away.

David wasn't fazed; he just gave me a lazy, sexy smile. "I'll call you soon," he said again and brushed his fingertips lightly against my breasts. My hard nipples were clearly visible through the sheer cotton of my sundress. I felt a slow burn rise in my face.

He quickly got into his car, started it up and put it into gear. "Bye, Gillian."

"Bye, David." I watched his blue convertible turn the corner and drive out of sight.

Over dinner, Mary studied me carefully. "David is certainly an attractive man . . . and he was certainly attracted to you. Are you going to go out with him?"

I shrugged, pretending nonchalance. "I gave him my phone number, but I'll doubt he'll call. He's a flirt—probably just likes to collect digits."

"Oh, I think he'll call," replied Mary. "And if you do go out with him, be very careful. You're in a vulnerable position right now, and David has a reputation."

"Reputation? What do you mean?"

Mary took a sip of her wine and fiddled with the glass stem. "I've heard gossip, and I see his name sometimes in the tabloids. After all, Wentworth Properties has made him very, very rich. He must be worth tens of millions."

I nearly dropped my fork. "Oh, my god, he's *that* David Wentworth? I never made the connection."

"Yes, he's that Wentworth. People say he's ruthless, used to getting what he wants by any means. And I heard that his divorce—I think it was about three years ago—was pretty messy."

"Well, thanks for the warning, Mary. I will be careful. I doubt anything will happen with this guy anyway. He must be used to having gorgeous women throw themselves at him."

"You're not the type to throw yourself at anyone, Gillian. I'm sure that's very appealing to David."

I thought of our passionate kiss in Ken and Jackie's driveway and fought hard to keep an embarrassed blush at bay. Thank God Mary hadn't witnessed that little scene.

That night I lay in bed, unable to sleep, my mind whirling. I thought about calling Anita—meeting David definitely fell into the "major news" category—but it was very late. And for some reason I wanted to keep this stunningly wonderful development to myself for a while.

I tossed and turned in bed for hours. I kept reliving every moment of our meeting—his electric-blue eyes and lazy smile, that unbelievable kiss. My heart was pounding. *Please, God, let him call me. . . . I have to see him again.*

Suddenly Miss Prudence and Miss Hornypants popped into my head. These two voices had first appeared during my adolescence, when my hormones and my good sense were constantly engaged in battle.

"*You acted like a complete slut,*" said Miss Prudence. "*Letting a stranger kiss you and touch your breasts—in public! What were you thinking?*"

"*He wasn't a complete stranger,*" Miss Hornypants pointed out. "*She'd known him a few hours.*"

"*A few hours!*" Miss Prudence was outraged.

"*It was just a kiss and a little fondling. It's not like she dropped to her knees and gave him a blow job.*"

"*It was bad enough! He probably thinks she's an easy piece of ass.*"

"*No, he doesn't. He was very attracted to her, and she felt the same way. Why pretend otherwise? They simply acted on their feelings.*"

"*She's going to regret—*"

"*Oh, both of you leave now!*" I demanded.

Once they had disappeared from my mind, I turned my thoughts back to David. What would he be like in bed? I immediately knew the answer: amazing.

I pulled my nightshirt all the way up to my neck. I closed my eyes and massaged my hard nipples, remembering David's fingers brushing gently against them. I imagined his lips and tongue on my breasts, kissing and licking, sucking and teasing . . . and then slowly making a wet trail down my stomach. . . . I imagined the roughness of his cheek against the soft skin of my thighs as he slowly parted them and lapped hungrily at my pussy . . . teasing my clit with the tip of his warm tongue. . . .

I felt an insistent ache growing between my thighs. My breathing quickened. I spread my legs and slowly rubbed my pussy lips together. I was very wet. I slid two fingers inside, imagining David's hard cock pumping into me, and rubbed my clit with my other hand. Within minutes I came intensely, convulsing and stifling a scream.

I didn't know it then, but it was the first of many incredible orgasms David would give me.

2

I drifted through Sunday, hoping David would call my cell, knowing he probably wouldn't. He didn't. I fought down disappointment and anxiety. *He will call me, he will call me . . .*

Mary drove me to the station to catch the 4:00 train. I hugged her hard. "Thanks for the great weekend, Mary, it was just what I needed."

"You can visit anytime, Gillian. And please remember what I said about David . . . I don't want to see you get hurt."

"Sure, I'll be careful." I didn't have the heart to tell her I had already fallen hard for this guy—physically anyway.

The train ride back to the city was blissful, especially compared to the ride out. I thought of David the whole way. I didn't think once about that other guy . . . what was his name . . . oh, right, Steve.

The city was still steaming hot. Nothing in my mailbox except a Visa bill with a $240 minimum payment due. Once I'd paid the bill and my rent, I'd have less than $300 in my checking account. I sighed as I realized I had to go back to temping.

I decided to lift my spirits by calling Anita. I gave her a blow-by-blow account of meeting David, leaving out only Aunt Mary's warning and my orgasmic sexual fantasy about him.

Anita gave a low whistle. "David Wentworth! He's quite a catch. Rich *and* good-looking. Elena Hernandez dated him for a few months."

"Oh, god, you mean that gorgeous Brazilian model who did the Revlon campaign? I can't compete with someone like her!" I squeaked.

"Elena is gorgeous, but she's also a mean bitch. It's no wonder he dumped her after a few months. And you're gorgeous, too, Gillian."

I snorted. "Yeah, right. At best I'm cute. But he probably won't call me anyway."

"Of course he will. And when he does, you have to let me know right away."

I laughed. "Okay . . . you'll be the first to know."

I hung up and started some desultory cleaning. I had the fan on at full blast but was soaked with sweat within minutes. God only knew when I'd have enough money to buy a new air conditioner.

My cell phone rang. *Anita again*, I thought, *with another tidbit of gossip about David*. "Hello?"

"Gillian? Hi, it's David Wentworth."

My knees turned so weak I had to sit down. I pushed a sweaty strand of hair out of my face. "Oh, hi, David, how are you?" I said in my best faux-casual voice.

"Fine, and you?"

"Fine." My palms were sweating, and I had to work hard to maintain a normal tone.

"I wondered if we could get together tomorrow night. Are you free?"

"Um, yes, I think so. I mean, yes, definitely."

"Great. I thought we could have dinner at Francesca's on Fifty-Second Street. Do you know it?"

"Oh, sure." Actually I'd only read about it—Francesca's was the new chic restaurant for celebrities and the super rich. I couldn't afford a cup of coffee at that place.

"I have a six P.M. meeting . . . do you mind meeting me there around eight?"

"Sure, that's fine." I felt relieved. I didn't want David to see my crappy apartment—or my crappy building or my crappy neighborhood, for that matter.

"Perfect. I'm really looking forward to seeing you again, Gillian."

"Me, too, David." We made small talk for a few minutes and then hung up. I was so proud that I'd managed to get through the conversation without sounding like Minnie Mouse or making a complete ass of myself.

I immediately dialed Anita's cell. "He called! We're having dinner tomorrow night at Francesca's."

She was almost as excited as I was. "That's fast work. He must be really into you. And dinner at Francesca's . . . he wants to impress you. What are you going to wear?"

"Oh, god, I hadn't even thought of that. I don't have anything good enough . . . what am I going to do?"

"Relax, your best friend is an expert at dealing with fashion emergencies. I have this really cute new Versace miniskirt that would look great on you."

"Anita, I can't fit into your clothes! I'm six inches shorter and twenty pounds heavier."

"Well, okay, we'll bag the miniskirt idea. But I can bring over accessories and makeup. I'll be there are soon as I can."

Twenty minutes later we were rummaging through my pathetic wardrobe. "What about this long green velvet dress?" Anita suggested. "You always look so pretty in it."

"Too formal and too hot. I usually wear it for family holiday gatherings."

"Okay . . . how about this blue suede suit?"

"Too businesslike."

Anita refused to be discouraged. "All right. How about the skirt from the blue suede suit with a pretty blouse? This white lace one has a nice low neckline—you definitely won't look too businesslike."

I tried on the outfit with strappy white high-heeled sandals. I was pleased until I turned around to get a rear view. "Oh, my god, my ass looks huge!"

"No, it doesn't," Anita disagreed firmly. "You have a great ass and great tits. I wish I had your assets . . . then I might actually have a shot at the *Victoria's Secret* catalog and the *Sports Illustrated* swimsuit issue."

I turned to look at her. She was dressed in faded jeans and an old T-shirt. No makeup. As usual, she looked spectacular. Anita had incredibly long, lean legs; Audrey Hepburn features; feline green eyes and short jet-black hair. It was impossible for her to look bad. I dismissed a twinge of jealousy.

"Okay, I'll trust your opinion. I'll wear this outfit. Now what about accessories?"

We finally agreed on her gold San Marco necklace and matching bracelet, with discreet gold hoop earrings. She also loaned me a white pashmina. She applied makeup and wrote down instructions so I could re-create the look the following night. When I studied myself in the mirror I felt like a princess—a much prettier, more sophisticated Gillian.

"Okay, just one last thing," said Anita. "Underwear."

"Anita, he's not going to see my underwear!"

"You never know." She smirked. "Besides, even if you don't end up in bed with him, pretty underwear will make you feel more confident."

"I guess so. . . . I do have a new bra and panty set I bought at Victoria's Secret. Aunt Mary gave me a gift certificate for my birthday." I showed her—a push-up bra and modest bikini panties in apricot silk trimmed with ivory lace.

"Perfect. You'll give David Wentworth the biggest hard-on of his life."

"Anita!" We collapsed into laughter.

It was nearly midnight when she left. "Now remember, I want to hear all the details right away. Have a wonderful time." She winked at me as she closed the front door behind her.

The following night I splurged on a taxi even though I couldn't afford it. I didn't want to take the subway or bus to Francesca's and dishevel my appearance. As I stood before the restaurant door, huge moths of nervous tension fluttered in my stomach. I closed my eyes and took three long, deep breaths, trying to center myself the way I did before going onstage or in front of a TV camera.

The hostess was a coolly elegant black woman in a low-cut ivory evening dress. "May I help you?" she asked with an imperious glance at me.

"Yes, I'm meeting David Wentworth."

"Of course. This way please." Her voice was a degree or two warmer, but her expression suggested that she still couldn't imagine what I was doing there.

"Gillian. You look wonderful." David rose and leaned over the table to peck my cheek. Even that brief contact was enough to make my heart race.

The hostess dropped a menu in front of me and then leaned far over the table to hand one to David. Her boobs nearly popped out of her gown. I glared at her. She ignored me. David seemed oblivious to the boob maneuver and my outrage.

We quickly ordered wine and entrees. I tried not to feel intimidated by the chandeliers, the priceless Persian rugs, the fine china and crystal.

David smiled and pinned me with his brilliant blue eyes. He was staring at me so intently I had to drop my gaze and fidget with my napkin to regain my composure.

"When I met you at Mary's I thought you looked familiar.... I'm wondering if I remember you from a commercial."

"Maybe. My most successful one was for Manhattan Bank. It ran for several months on local stations. I played Satisfied Customer Number One."

"Yes, I remember now. You were excellent as a satisfied customer."

The mild sexual innuendo was enough to make me blush ferociously.

"So how was your meeting?" I asked to change the subject.

"Pretty good. I'm working on a new luxury condo project in Boston. There's been a lot of red tape, a lot of problems with subcontractors, but we're making progress."

Our entrees arrived. My salmon dish was mind-blowing—what Anita and I called "ohmigod food"—but I was too nervous to enjoy it. David and I chatted casually about our backgrounds. I told him about growing up in rural New Hampshire with Anita; he talked about Denver and his childhood dream of becoming a professional tennis player. A severe knee injury had ended his budding career.

Two hours slipped by; eventually we were the only customers left in the restaurant. David sat back in his chair and again mesmerized me with his gaze. "I just moved into a new apartment on East Seventy-Fifth Street. I'd love to show it to you."

I felt a moment of panic. Miss Prudence and Miss Hornypants made a brief appearance in my head.

"He wants to have sex with you! You never sleep with a man on the first date!" cried Miss Prudence.

"Go for it. You might not get a second chance with this guy," urged Miss Hornypants.

Miss H. won. "I'd love to see your apartment."

"Great. My car and driver are just outside." He leaned across the table and softly kissed my lips. My panties were soaked. I knew I was about to experience the most intense sexual pleasure of my life.

No ostentatious stretch limo for David. His car was a sleek black Mercedes with tinted windows. "Gillian, this is Al," he said, introducing me to the driver. Al, a huge, swarthy middle-aged guy, opened the back door for me and grinned. I liked him immediately.

In the car David chatted with Al about sports. Taking my fingers in a firm grip, he moved my hand to his thigh. I could feel his potent body heat; I swallowed hard.

The elegant lobby of his apartment building had the hushed atmosphere of a European museum. In the elevator David punched the PH button and then kissed me hard, slowly sliding his tongue between my lips. He ran his hands down my back to my ass. By then my nipples were rising and my pussy was aching. When the elevator doors opened he released me.

"Would you like the grand tour of the apartment?" he asked.

No, I want you to rip off my clothes and take me right here in the foyer. I restrained myself. "Yes, I'd love a tour."

The living/dining area was about the size of a football field. Huge floor-to-ceiling windows revealed a stunning panorama of the East River. The decor was muted and elegant—steel-gray leather sofas and ottomans; large Cubist paintings that appeared to be Picasso originals; a few enormous floral arrangements in crystal vases. I'd seen apartments like this only in *House Beautiful* and *Architectural Digest*. "It's lovely," I murmured, trying not to let my impatience show.

He took my hand and pulled me through the kitchen, the study, the guest room, and finally to the master bedroom. I was disappointed when the tour didn't stop there; I was about to expire from frustrated lust. He showed me the master bathroom and then led me into his dressing room. There he finally kissed me again; I could feel his heart pounding. "Give me your tongue," he demanded. I obeyed.

As he slowly unbuttoned my blouse I reached down to massage the bulge straining at his fly. His cock was extremely hard—and apparently extremely large. I glanced to the right and understood why we were starting here. A full-length mirror on his closet door reflected everything we did to each other. It was incredibly exciting to watch.

David pulled off my blouse and expertly unhooked my bra. "God, Gillian, your breasts are beautiful," he breathed. "So round and firm . . . and your nipples . . ." He began to lick and suck; it was even better than my fantasy. My nipples looked like raspberries.

I dropped to my knees and unzipped his fly. I pulled out his straining cock and flicked my tongue over the head, teasing out drops of cum. David groaned. I pulled down his pants and briefs and then attacked his shaft and balls with my lips and tongue. His balls were very tight. David's breathing quickened as he watched me in the mirror. "Gillian, please stop. . . . It feels wonderful, but I don't want to go off too soon."

"Oh, no, we definitely don't want that." I gave him a mischievous smile as I stretched out on the floor. David yanked off his remaining clothes and dropped down next to me. He pulled off my sandals and lifted my skirt. I spread my legs for him, wet and ready, but he made me wait. He gently stroked my pussy through my panties.

"David . . . how did you know how much I love that? My pussy is dripping."

He smiled, slid a finger under the elastic and deep inside me. "My god, you are so wet. . . ." He stripped off my panties and spread my lips. "And your clit is so swollen. . . ." He started licking and sucking; I felt the deep throb of a building orgasm. "Please let me come, please. . . ." I whimpered.

He pulled away. "Not yet, darling, not yet." He stroked my lips lightly with his pinky finger.

"I want your tongue again. . . . Please lick my pussy," I moaned.

He blew his warm breath over my engorged clit, bringing me so close to the edge.

"Please, David, *please*. . . ."

He plunged his tongue deep into my hole and pressed his thumb against my clit.

I came hard, harder than I ever had before. As I lay there gasping, David slowly stroked his cock and stared at my pussy. When I had recovered enough, he knelt between my knees and thrust hard into me. I whimpered. He began to pump slowly and then faster as I gyrated beneath him. I screamed as I came again, digging my nails into his shoulders. He suddenly pulled his cock out, groaned my name and spurted hot cum all over my breasts.

We lay there for a few minutes, trying to slow our ragged breathing and racing hearts. "God, Gillian," he said, "I knew sex would be good with you, but I had no idea. . . ."

"That I was such a lusty wench?"

He laughed. "Lusty wenches are my favorite kind of woman. Seriously, you're amazing."

"Oh, David," I whispered. "I have so many fantasies. . . ."

"I know, darling," he whispered back. "And I want to make them all come true."

I straddled him and pressed his free hand against my pussy. "Make me come again, David." I squeezed my legs around his thigh and rocked as fast as I could, feeling his finger slide deep into my ass. Intense pleasure built to a crescendo and burst through my body; from a distance I could hear myself scream.

I was limp and panting as David pulled my legs apart and slid his cock inside me. I sat perfectly still on his cock for a few minutes and then started to rock slowly again, staring at his glistening shaft as it slid in and out of my pussy. "I want you to come hard," I murmured. "I want you to explode deep inside me. I want to watch your hot cum dripping out of my pussy."

"Yes . . . I'm going to give it to you. . . ." David suddenly grabbed my ass and squeezed my cheeks hard. I tightened my pussy muscles around his cock and rocked harder. David dug his fingers into my ass cheeks as he came with a long groan.

We made love two more times that night, sharing the intimate secrets of our bodies. We quickly learned the best ways to tease, please and satisfy each other. We both loved oral sex, so the sixty-nine position was especially exciting for us. David straddled my face and bent over to lap at my pussy as I licked his balls and sucked hard on the head of his cock. The moment I came, I felt his cum gushing into my mouth and down my throat.

Happily aching and sated, I slept deeply in his antique four-poster bed. When I woke up late the next morning, I was stunned and disappointed to find myself alone. "David?" I called tentatively.

He entered the bedroom from the dressing room. He was buttoning a crisp white dress shirt. "Good morning, Gillian," he said briskly. "I hope you slept well. Unfortunately I have to run because I'm late for a meeting. There's coffee in the kitchen if you want some. . . ." He looked away from me, intent on inserting gold cuff links in his cuffs.

I wasn't going to allow him to get away so easily. "That's too bad, David." I sighed. "Because I'm feeling incredibly horny this morning."

I flung back the bedspread to reveal my hard nipples. David stopped fidgeting with the cuff links and stared.

"I guess I'll just have to masturbate. And I'd much rather have your hard cock." I slowly spread my legs and then my pussy lips. I gently rubbed my clit with a finger.

"Gillian, I really have to go—" His voice was hesitant.

I looked at the growing bulge in his pants. "But you don't want to," I whispered as I slid two fingers inside my pussy.

"Oh, god." He dropped the cuff links.

I felt triumphant.

He unzipped his fly and pulled out his rock-hard shaft.

"How do you want to fuck me, David?"

"From behind. Kneel on the edge of the bed."

I obeyed, exposing my ass and my wet pussy to him. He thrust into me hard and deep and then remained still for a moment. I looked around and saw him massaging his balls, his eyes half closed in bliss.

"Play with my clit while you fuck me," I demanded. I felt his warm fingers massaging my lips and then stroking my clit with a featherlight touch. "Fuck me now, fuck me as hard as you can."

He pumped his shaft in and out as he increased the pressure on my clit. "I love to fuck you, Gillian. . . . I love to make you scream. . . ."

I bit my knuckles and released a long howl as he shouted my name. I felt his cum spurting into my pussy as I collapsed onto my stomach, overwhelmed by pleasure.

3

Forty-five minutes later David rushed out the door, yelling, "I'll call you soon," over his shoulder. I took another hot shower in his cavernous bathroom, luxuriating in steam and memories of his hands and tongue, his hot breath in my ear . . . I didn't think I could possibly come again so soon, but I leaned against the warm marble and massaged my clit until I moaned with a long, shuddering release.

The subway ride home should have been a jarring dose of reality, but I was too stupefied by pleasure. I sat there in a blissful daze, unable to stop smiling. "High at this time in the morning . . . disgraceful," snorted an elderly woman on my right. I just giggled.

I was so distracted I missed my stop. I didn't care. I nearly skipped the twelve blocks home.

I called Anita on my cell. "How was it? What's he really like? Did you hit it off? Did you sleep with him? Are you going to see him again?" She fired questions at me until I laughed.

"Meet me at Java Java in twenty minutes, and I'll tell you all . . . well, nearly all."

* * *

I leaned over the table and whispered, "So he stayed even though he was late for his meeting. The sex was even better than it had been the night before. I've never had sex like that. He was so turned on it really excited me."

"I'm so glad for you, Gillian . . . and a little jealous." Anita sighed and polished off her latte. "Sex with Michael has become routine. Half the time he doesn't seem very interested. I'm beginning to wonder if he's cheating on me. These frigging fashion photographers are so spoiled. Some of them try to lay every model they meet, and most of the time they succeed."

"Dump him, Anita! You could find another guy in five seconds flat."

"Maybe. But could I find a great guy like David Wentworth? You're so lucky. When are you going to see him again?"

"Not sure . . . he said he'd call me soon." I felt a sudden plunging sensation in my stomach. *I'll call you soon*—the lame kiss-off so many men used. "Oh, god, Anita, what if he doesn't? I mean, I fucked his brains out on the first date. Maybe that's all he wanted, a hot one-night stand—"

"Don't think like that," Anita scolded. "If the sex was that great he'll be back for more. Besides, you have a lot to offer. I'll bet he's interested in you, not just your body."

"I don't know." I felt overwhelmed with doubt. "But there's nothing I can do about it. Waiting for his call might just kill me."

"It's time for serious distraction." Anita scooped up her purse and stood. "Let's go shopping. There's a great new secondhand boutique down the street. They have all kinds of cool stuff from the fifties and sixties."

"All right. I can't afford anything, but at least I can look."

Anita persuaded me to buy a sheer black lace blouse for $20. "Don't wear a bra underneath. . . . It will drive David crazy," she said.

"You're a shameless vixen." I laughed. "I do want him to notice my personality, not just my bouncing boobs."

"Trust me, you'll have his full attention if you wear that blouse."

"Let's get out of here before I'm tempted to spend more money I don't have."

We ambled down West Fourteenth Street, enjoying the warm sunshine and cool breeze. The heat and humidity had finally broken; it was possible to walk three blocks without ending up drenched in sweat.

Anita suddenly gasped and grabbed my arm. I followed her stare. Across the street two men were emerging from Antonio's, a hot new gay bar. The cute blond guy looked very familiar. . . . "Oh, my god, it's Steve," I whispered. The other man was a tall, slender young Asian. Anita and I watched in shock as the two men embraced and briefly kissed. I nearly passed out.

"Hey, Steve!" yelled Anita. He turned around with a startled look. Anita pulled my arm and dragged me to the opposite curb. "Steve, I haven't seen you in so long," she cooed. "Aren't you going to introduce us to your friend?"

I didn't think anyone could blush more deeply than I could, but Steve surpassed me. He resembled a tomato with sunburn. "Uh, hi, Anita, Gillian," he stammered. "This is my friend Oliver."

I didn't know what to say beyond a mumbled "hello." Anita ratcheted up the sarcasm. "How nice to meet you, Oliver. You and Steve look so cute together. Have you known each other long?"

"Just a few weeks."

Oliver looked baffled; he clearly had no clue about what was going on.

"Anita!" I hissed.

She ignored me. "And where did you meet?"

"On the set of *Nights of Passion*. I'm a new writer for the show." Oliver looked increasingly uncomfortable. Steve was staring at the pavement.

"Anita, we really should go. Nice to meet you, Oliver; good to see you, Steve," I babbled. I yanked Anita's arm and dragged her away.

As soon as we turned the corner, we looked at each other and burst into laughter. "Well, that explains a lot," said Anita. "No wonder Steve didn't enjoy sex with you—you don't have a penis!"

This set us off again. I wiped tears from my eyes. "I had absolutely no clue. It's quite a shock . . . but at least I found out fairly soon. I mean, what if I'd found out after a year or two?"

"Or after you got engaged or married. . . . That happened to an Italian model I worked with in Paris. She was devastated."

"And just think . . . if Steve hadn't dumped me when he did, I never would have hooked up with David."

"You have good karma, Gillian. Things always work out for the best for you."

The surprises weren't over. A few hours later my cell phone rang, and I answered immediately, convinced it was David. It was the last person I had expected—Steve.

"Gillian . . . look . . . I just wanted to explain. . . ."

I didn't know how to respond, or even how to feel. I felt torn between anger, surprise, amusement, and sympathy.

"Were you sleeping with men while you were dating me?" I asked abruptly.

"No, I swear it. Look, the truth is that I've always been attracted to men, but I've tried to fight it. You know my background, Gillian. My parents are right-wing Christians . . . not exactly gay friendly. I thought I could be happy with the right woman. And I did care about you, Gillian. You know that's true."

I did know. "Okay. I'm still stunned by all of this, but I understand. Sort of."

Steve released a sigh. "Thanks, Gillian. I felt like such a shit when I broke up with you. I thought about explaining everything to you that night, but I decided it would just make things worse."

"You're right, it probably would have. But how are you going to deal with your parents?"

"I'm visiting them in Virginia next month, and I'll come out then. If they can't accept me . . . well, that will be their problem. I can't keep lying anymore."

"Good luck, Steve. You have a lot to offer, and Oliver is lucky to have you."

"Thanks, Gillian. I hope you meet a great guy soon."

"Actually I already have. I met David Wentworth at Aunt Mary's house and I've been dating him." I felt and sounded more than a little smug.

"David Wentworth! Way to go, Gillian!" He sounded genuinely glad and genuinely impressed.

"Well, we've only had one date, but we really hit it off."

"If he's smart, he'll hang on to you. There aren't many women like you around, Gillian."

"Thanks. It's nice to be appreciated, even by a gay ex-boyfriend. Now tell me more about Oliver. He's very cute."

Steve gushed like a thirteen-year-old with his first crush. I felt really happy for him. It was hard to believe that I could feel this way after the devastation I'd experienced just a week before.

Steve and I agreed to get together for lunch. I hung up the phone and continued the endless wait for the one call that would make me happy.

4

David softly stroked my inner thigh. "I'm going to make you so wet, Gillian," he whispered. "I'm going to tease you until you're hot and excited and begging for my hard cock. Then I'm going to pump it into you, slowly at first, and then faster—I'm going to make you come over and over again. And when I'm ready to come I'm going to pull my cock out and spurt all over your breasts. . . . Then I'll straddle your face so you can lick my balls and suck the head of my cock until I'm hard again. . . ."

"Gillian? Gillian? *Gillian!*"

I was rudely awakened from my fantasy. "I'm sorry, Mr. Conley. What can I do for you?" I shifted uncomfortably in my chair to relieve the tingling between my legs. I now understood the agony felt by guys with unexpected public hard-ons.

Mr. Conley looked impatient and irritable, as always. "Please take this file up to Ms. Johnson on the twenty-fifth floor. It's urgent."

"Of course, I'll do it right away." As I took the file from him I felt like a zombie and probably looked like one, too. I'd temped as a receptionist at this accounting firm before, it ranked high on my list of mind-numbing jobs.

After dropping off the file, I ducked into the ladies' room. I couldn't stand it any longer; I had to get some relief. I locked myself in a stall and unbuttoned my blouse. I pulled down my bra and rubbed my thumbs over my nipples until they stiffened. I was breathing hard, thinking of David's large hands cupping and gently squeezing my breasts. I pulled up my skirt and slid my hand down my panty hose. I rubbed my pussy through my panties and felt the deep throbbing intensify. I slipped my fingers under the elastic and caressed my swollen clit, slowly at first and then harder and faster . . . *David's cock, pumping harder and faster* . . . and I came so hard it was almost painful. I pressed my other hand against my mouth to stifle my scream.

"Anita, I don't know what to do. It's been nearly a week and David hasn't called. I've almost given up. I guess it was just a one-night stand. I know I shouldn't care so much, but I'm really disappointed."

"Come on, he's a very busy guy. I'm sure he'll call. I'll bet he's been thinking about you as much as you've been thinking about him."

I laughed weakly. "Yeah, right. I guess I should be glad I had that one night with him. It's something to remember when I'm old and decrepit."

"I still think you shouldn't give up. But let's do something fun this weekend to take your mind off him. How about a club Saturday night?"

"Sure, sounds good," I replied, trying to sound enthusiastic. "Thanks for listening, Anita. Give me a call later this week, and we'll get together Saturday night."

I hung up and puttered around the apartment, trying to force David out of my mind.

"*What did you expect?*" sniped Miss Prudence. "*Of course*

he's not going to call. He got what he wanted from you—and it was way too easy."

"He was very hot for you, and he still is," countered Miss Hornypants. *"He wants to see you again. Why sit around waiting for his call? You can call him."*

This obvious fact startled me out of my reverie. Of course I could call him—why hadn't I thought of it earlier? If he blew me off, it would be embarrassing, but at least I'd know where things stood.

I picked up my cell phone and flipped it open. Then I remembered—I didn't have his phone number.

"He never gave it to you—a good sign that he had no interest in seeing you again." Miss Prudence sounded smug.

"Maybe not. After all, you never asked him for his number," Miss Hornypants pointed out. *"You could call his office."*

Another brilliant suggestion from Miss H. For some reason I always ended up following her advice and ignoring Miss P.

I flipped open the phone book and found Wentworth Properties. My palms sweated as I punched in the number. I negotiated my way through the automated directory and finally reached a human. "David Wentworth, please," I stammered. I half expected the operator to decline my request, but she immediately connected me. I braced myself, waiting for the sound of David's voice.

"David Wentworth's office. Elizabeth Stone speaking," said an efficient feminine voice.

"Oh . . . hi. I'd like to speak to David Wentworth, please."

"Mr. Wentworth is out of town. I'm his assistant. May I help you?"

"Um, no. I'm just a friend. Do you know when he'll be back?"

"I'm sorry, his plans are uncertain. May I take a message?"

"Uhhh . . . no message. I'll just try again next week."

I hung up abruptly. David had gone out of town without even

telling me. That was it. He definitely didn't want to see me again. I closed my eyes and bit my lip, trying to push away the waves of disappointment and humiliation. *Just let it go, Gillian . . . just move on.*

It was close to midnight, but I still couldn't sleep. I turned the light on and picked up the latest Sue Grafton mystery. Kinsey Millhone was a woman facing *real* problems. I became completely absorbed in her story.

When my cell phone rang I nearly jumped out of my skin. Who could be calling so late? Probably Anita or someone calling the wrong number.

I flipped open the phone. "Hi, it's Gillian." I yawned.

"Gillian, it's David."

I nearly said, "David who?" A split second later, I sat bolt upright. "David! It's so great to hear from you," I gushed.

"I'm sorry to call so late. I've been in Boston all week, dealing with this damned condo project." He sounded very tired.

"That's okay, I understand. I was awake when you called." I felt flushed with happiness.

"I've been thinking about you a lot, Gillian. And I get hard every time I think of you."

"Really?"

"Really. That night with you—and that morning—was incredible."

"Yes, it was. I've been thinking about you, too," I purred.

"I'm coming back to New York tomorrow night. My flight gets in pretty late, but I thought I could pick you up on the way from the airport to my apartment—"

"Yes!" I blurted out.

David laughed. His laughter was so rare it felt like a triumph every time I coaxed it from him. "I look forward to it. I'll see you tomorrow night," he said.

"Wait, David." I didn't want the conversation to end so quickly. "I thought you might like to know what I'm wearing right now—a black silk teddy with red lace." (I was actually wearing a faded pink cotton nightshirt with a large coffee stain on the front.)

"Gillian . . ." His breathing deepened and quickened.

"Are you hard right now, David?"

"Extremely hard."

"Good. I want you to take your cock out and stroke it for me."

I waited a moment. He gave a little groan. "I'm stroking it. God, I wish you were here."

"So do I. I've pulled the top of my teddy down. . . . I'm playing with my hard nipples. . . ."

"Oh, darling, I wish I could see you. . . ."

"Hold on, I'm going to take the teddy off completely. There. I'm spreading my legs . . . and now my lips. My pussy is very warm and wet. If you were here right now, what would you do to me?"

His breathing was ragged. "I'd run my tongue all over your body . . . from your throat down to your breasts and then across your belly to your sweet pussy. I'd kiss your pussy and tease your clit with my tongue. . . ."

"David, I want you so much." I felt completely out of control. My fingers were wet with my juice. "I want your cock in me. I want you to explode in my pussy . . . I want your cum. Give it to me, David . . . give me all of your cum. . . ." A cry burst from my throat as he let out a long, deep moan. For a minute the only sound was our harsh breathing.

"Oh, that was good." I sighed. "Did you like it?"

"I loved it. Gillian, I have to go now. I'll see you tomorrow night. I'll call you on my way from the airport." His tone was suddenly abrupt and distant.

"Oh, okay." I tried to hide the disappointment in my voice. *He's tired*, I told myself. "Good night, David. I look forward to tomorrow night."

I turned off the light and tried to sleep, but once again thoughts of David kept me awake. I was so excited at the prospect of seeing him again—and nervous. He was a complicated man. I'd have to handle him very carefully.

5

"He called, he called, he called," I sang to Anita over the phone the next morning.

"Ha! I knew it! When will you see him again?"

"Tonight. He's been in Boston working on a condo project. He's going to pick me up on his way home from the airport."

"Sounds like he can't wait. You've gotten under his skin, girl."

"I don't know about that." I sighed. "Sometimes he seems really into me, but other times he seems so distant."

"Hey, come on, you've known each other such a short time. Guys are always wary at this stage."

"I know, but he's so different from the other men I've dated. I feel like I have to handle him with kid gloves."

"Well, that's not a bad idea. But just try to relax a bit. David is handsome, smart, rich and he has a tremendous passion for you. Most women would kill to be in your position. So enjoy it."

"Maybe you're right." I laughed. "I guess you could give Dr. Phil and Dr. Laura a run for their money."

"Of course I'm right. Let's meet tomorrow at Java Java for a dish session."

After we agreed to meet at four P.M., I hung up. Anita *was* right, I decided. I should just enjoy my time with David . . . for as long as it lasted.

"Hi, Gillian, we're about five minutes from your place," said David.

"Okay, I'll be waiting in the foyer," I said breathlessly. "See you soon."

I hung up and gave myself a last glance in the mirror. I was wearing my new black lace blouse with no bra underneath. Anita was right; it did look incredibly sexy. I gave a silent prayer of thanks to the goddess of round, firm breasts.

I threw on a short black jacket. I was also wearing a short black skirt and sheer thigh-high stockings with black suede pumps. I'd once worn a similar outfit for Steve, but he hadn't responded in the way I had hoped. I had a feeling David's reaction would be more enthusiastic.

I rushed downstairs to the foyer and looked through the glass door for David's car. As soon as the sleek Mercedes pulled up, I ran out. Al emerged from the driver's side and opened the back door for me. I slid in and felt David's arms crushing me to his chest. He gave me a deep kiss, his tongue intertwining with mine. When Al slid back into the driver's seat, I pulled my mouth away, feeling self-conscious. I kept my arms around David's neck. "I've missed you," I whispered.

A brief silence that seemed to last forever. "I've missed you, too," David finally replied. *Damn, I'm scaring him,* I thought. I distracted his attention from the awkward moment by skimming my hands down to his broad chest. His heart was pounding. He slid his hands under my jacket and teased my nipples into hardness. I covered his neck with urgent kisses, ending with a gentle bite. He moved one hand from my breast to my thigh, creeping slowly up to my panties. I felt a warm, throbbing ache in my pussy as he stroked my clit through the silk.

The car stopped abruptly, making us lurch forward. "Sorry," said Al. "That cab cut me off."

I had completely forgotten Al's presence. Embarrassed, I pulled David's hand away, closed my legs and sat up straight. David seemed more amused than annoyed by my sudden primness.

In the elevator I gave up any attempt at propriety. As soon as the doors closed, David dropped to his knees and lifted my skirt. I held it up as he pulled down my panties and buried his tongue between my pussy lips. "Oh, my god," I moaned. I ground my pussy against his face as he licked my clit harder. I came before we reached the tenth floor.

When the elevator doors opened we stumbled into the foyer, delirious with lust. David quickly stripped me in front of the ornate mirror, leaving on my thigh-high stockings and suede pumps. "Come over here." He pulled me into the living room and sat me down on a large leather ottoman. "Spread your legs. I want to look at your pussy while you suck my cock."

In the past I'd always been annoyed by men who gave orders, but for some reason David's urgency was a turn-on. I wanted to obey him. He stood in front of me as I opened my thighs and unzipped his fly. I pulled out his engorged cock and held it firmly in both hands. I gave the head a featherlight lick.

"Do you like that? Do you want more?" I asked. Two could play at the domination game.

"Yes, I like it. I want more; please give me more. . . ." he pleaded.

I gave the head a second light lick and then another, just a bit longer and harder. With one hand I massaged his balls. I licked and sucked the head, increasing the intensity until he was on the brink of coming. I stopped abruptly.

"What do you want now, David?"

"I want to put my cock in your pussy. I want to fuck you until you scream with pleasure. . . ."

He fell to his knees. I wrapped my hand around his shaft and rubbed the head against my clit until I was dripping wet again. "Now," I said. "Fuck me now."

He thrust his cock in, making me moan with delight. He stayed perfectly still for a moment and then started a long, slow rhythm. I put my hands on his ass, pulling him in deeper. "Harder. Fuck me harder. Make me come again," I demanded.

He thrust harder. I closed my eyes as I felt the orgasm build. I bucked and convulsed, crying out loud as David shuddered and moaned.

As he pulled his cock out of me I fell backward on the ottoman. "Oh, god, that was amazing." I sighed.

"For me, too."

"And that was a very nice surprise in the elevator. Was it an impulse, or have you been fantasizing about doing that to me?"

"Oh, I've been fantasizing about it for days."

I suddenly bolted upright. "Oh, my god, David!"

"What's wrong?"

"The security camera in the elevator! We must have been filmed. Oh, Jesus, I can't believe it—"

David laughed. "Relax, honey. I called the security guard from the airport and told him to turn off the camera for a few hours."

"And you think he did it?"

"I'm sure of it. After all, I do own the building."

"Oh." I flopped back down on the ottoman, feeling relieved but also a little intimidated. At times I forgot just how rich and powerful David was.

"Shall we move to the bedroom?" he suggested.

"In a minute," I replied lazily. "Right now I'd like you to . . ." I paused, overcome by a moment of shyness.

"What would you like, darling?" David was kneeling beside the ottoman, staring at me intently. "You can share any fantasy with me. I won't be shocked. I'd love to please you."

"I want you to . . ." I paused for another moment.

"Go on," he coaxed.

"I want you to put your fingers in my pussy and rub your cum all over my breasts."

"Yes . . . I'd like that, too." I felt his long, supple fingers enter my pussy. As he smeared the warm cum all over my breasts I watched my nipples rise at his touch. He moved his hand back to my pussy and then slid three fingers in my mouth. I tasted his salty sweet cum.

"God, you're such a sexy little thing. . . ."

"I'm not always like this, " I murmured. "You make me this way. You make me horny and wet. . . ."

"And you make me horny and hard." David took my hand, pulled me to my feet and led me to the bedroom.

He stood by the bed, stroking his cock into hardness as he watched me fondle my breasts and lick the cum off my hard nipples. Then I spread my legs and my lips for him, playing with my clit and sliding my fingers inside my pussy.

"Let's sixty-nine again," he whispered. "But I want you on top this time." He stretched out on the bed, and I lowered my pussy over his mouth. I leaned down and grasped his hard shaft in one hand, kissing the head. I felt his tongue flickering over my lips and my clit and then sliding up the crack of my ass. I was delighted by a new and exquisite sensation as he parted my cheeks and licked my hole. I stroked his shaft and sucked hard on the head. His tongue finally slid from my ass back to my pussy. He lapped hard at my clit until I came intensely, my cries muffled by the big cock in my mouth. I squeezed his shaft and felt it convulse as the cum burst into my mouth.

* * *

I woke up the next morning to find David sitting next to me on the bed. "Good morning," he said, looking way too bright and alert. He slowly pulled the sheet down from my neck.

"Mmmph," I replied and stretched slowly. David trailed his fingers across my breasts, down along my belly and lightly over my pussy. He gently spread my legs and caressed my lips and clit. "My god, you're so wet," he whispered. "You must have been dreaming about sex."

"Yes," I murmured, undulating slowly under his touch. "Sometimes I come in my sleep."

"I think you came last night."

"Yes . . . and you're going to make me come again this morning."

David smiled. "But not yet, darling. I want you to wait."

He removed his hand from my pussy, which made me wince with frustration. He straddled my face and took his rock-hard cock in his fist. I watched as he stroked until droplets of cum oozed from the head. He rubbed the head against my mouth; I licked the drops of cum from my lips. When I opened my mouth he slid the shaft all the way in. He reached back with one hand and played with my clit as he slowly pumped his cock in and out of my mouth. I held back as long as I could, finally moaning around his shaft as I came. I felt his cock convulse, and a burst of hot cum flowed down my throat.

"God, Gillian, that was incredible." David fell back against the pillows. "I wish we could go for another round, but I'm late again for the office."

I put my arms around his neck and snuggled against his chest. "I thought you were the boss man. Can't you be as late as you want to be?"

He smiled, but his voice was a little tense. "Sure, I could, but if I don't get in at a reasonable hour, things pile up. . . ." He gently disengaged my arms and stood up.

I felt a pinprick of anger and disappointment. *Play it cool,*

Gillian. "Oh, well." I shrugged. "Maybe sometime we can spend the entire day in bed."

"I'd love that." David leaned over the bed and gave me a quick kiss. Damn, this guy knew how to turn me on, piss me off and appease me in the space of minutes.

"Sounds like it's going really well." Anita slurped at her latte.

"I suppose it is. I just wish he weren't so distant sometimes. Well, I guess there's always something to complain about. He did give me his cell-phone number so I won't have to sit around waiting in agony for him to call."

"That's definitely a step in the right direction. And he's obviously doing everything right in bed. You look great. You have the radiant glow of a well-fucked woman."

"Anita!"

"Well, it's true. Cosmetic companies have been trying to bottle and sell that glow for years. David's giving it to you for free. "

"For as long as our affair lasts. It does feel like an affair, even though he's not married."

"Even better. Much more exciting than a boring relationship."

"I suppose so." I took a bite of cranberry scone and wondered why I still felt so uncertain.

The next day I got a phone call from Ellen, my eternally optimistic agent. For once she had genuine good news. "Honey, you got a callback for the radio-station commercial," she gushed. "That's going to be a major campaign. I'm sure you're going to get it. And there's a part on *Law & Order* that would be perfect for you." I took down the info for the *Law & Order* audition and the callback, trying not to let her enthusiasm inflate my expectations to unrealistic levels.

But I felt a new confidence and determination. I nailed the

callback and landed the radio commercial. My euphoria helped me float through the *Law & Order* audition. I screamed with joy when Ellen called to tell me I'd gotten that part as well.

I had to share the news with David. I called his cell and felt a little let down when I got his voice mail, but I left a message, and he called me back within twenty minutes.

"Gillian, that's great. I'm so glad for you," he said. "*Law & Order* is a terrific show."

"Well, my part isn't big, but it's juicy. I play the grief-stricken sister of a murder victim. Of course there are plot twists—turns out the sister isn't so grief-stricken after all."

"Sounds wonderful."

"It's a helluva lot better than the last role I had on that show. About six years ago I played a corpse. A crack whore's corpse. I was on screen for about seven seconds."

That made him laugh. "I'm sure you were an exceptional corpse, but we should celebrate your new success. I'd love to see you tomorrow night. Are you available?"

"Gosh, I'll have to check my appointment book. I have so many handsome, sexy men chasing me it's hard to keep my dates straight."

He laughed again. I felt another moment of victory. We agreed to meet at Francesca's. The familiar tingle of anticipation rushed through my body.

6

For the next few weeks, everything was blissful. I saw David frequently. I expected the sex to slow down and cool off, but every time was more exciting than the last.

I lost nine pounds without even thinking about it. One night as I lay on the floor in front of the dressing-room mirror, David ran his hand from my pussy to my breasts. "Honey, you look great . . . your stomach and your tits . . . but don't lose any more weight. I like your curves."

"Sir, yes, sir." I laughed.

Francesca's became our favorite rendezvous. I became accustomed to the elegant atmosphere; even the snooty hostess no longer intimidated me. One night I impulsively decided to be daring. As we waited for the check, I excused myself and went to the ladies' room. When I returned, I slid into my chair and told David I had a present for him. He raised his eyebrows in surprise. I slowly pulled my red lace panties out of my purse.

"I thought you might like these," I said, slipping them under the table to him. "Just looking at you makes me so horny . . . I played with myself in the ladies' room. And now I'm extremely wet."

"Gillian . . ." His eyes glazed over with the look of lust that had become so familiar to me.

I scooted my chair closer to him. "If you're very careful and discreet, you can touch me under the table," I whispered.

He reached under the tablecloth and slid his hand up the thigh-high stockings he liked me to wear. His deft fingers fluttered inside my thigh and over my lips and swollen clit. I had to bite my lip to suppress a moan. I leaned forward and pressed my hand against his crotch. His hard-on was huge.

"David, I want you so much. . . ."

"I want you, too, Gillian." His voice was hoarse.

I rubbed his hard-on. "Do you have a favorite position, David?"

"Yes . . . I like to enter you from behind."

I flicked my tongue briefly across his throat. "I like that position, too. Doggy style. Woof."

"Excuse me, sir." The waiter was standing there with a completely impassive expression on his face. David and I jumped apart. My face flamed, but David was unperturbed as he signed the receipt.

I was so embarrassed I wanted to leave as quickly as possible, but David just smiled. "I need to relax for a moment, Gillian. I'm a little too excited."

That made me giggle. "Sorry. I hope I didn't make you too uncomfortable."

"It's worth the pain, darling." He took my panties from his lap and briefly rubbed them against his cheek before slipping them into his jacket pocket. Then he leaned forward to give me a long, slow kiss. It was the prelude to another incredible night.

As soon as we entered the foyer of his apartment, I dropped to my knees and upzipped his fly. I pulled out his shaft and gave the head several long, slow licks. I sucked the head as hard as I could while I stroked the shaft.

"Gillian, please . . . you're going to make me come too quickly. . . ."

I stopped sucking for a moment and stared up at him. His face was contorted with the effort to stay in control.

"I want you to come," I murmured. "I want you to shoot a big load into my mouth. And when you're done, you'll satisfy me with your tongue."

I sucked the head again even harder. David grasped my hair and plunged his shaft deep, crying out as the cum shot into my mouth. I swallowed.

"Now it's my turn." I stood and pushed him to his knees. I pulled up my skirt and pressed my pussy against his lips. He kissed and licked my pussy lips and then sucked gently on my clit.

"Fuck me with your fingers while you suck my clit," I panted.

He slid three fingers inside my hot, wet hole. The ache in my pussy intensified until it was almost unbearable. I finally convulsed around his fingers. He slowly removed his fingers from my pussy and licked off the cum.

Mary came to the city and took me out for lunch at a lovely café near Central Park West. I chattered happily about my booming career as we attacked our grilled salmon salads.

"Of course the *Law & Order* part was a one-off, but I think I made a real impression. The commercial shoot went well, too. Ellen told me the radio station is planning a second commercial, and they want me again. They're probably going to use shots from the commercials for print ads and billboards as well."

Mary beamed at me. "I'm so happy for you, Gillian. I knew you'd make it if you just hung in there."

"Well, God knows I've come close to giving up. I can't tell

you the number of times I've nearly thrown in the towel and moved back to Hanson. But I kept thinking, what the hell would I do in Hanson? I can't imagine pursuing any career but acting."

"I know it sounds corny, but you followed your heart, and now you're reaping the benefits. Speaking of your heart . . . how's your love life these days? I've been hoping you and Steve would get back together."

I glanced away from her sharp blue eyes. "Well, no. I'm afraid it's never going to work with Steve." I gave her a quick explanation.

Mary looked surprised. "I never thought Steve might be gay. It's a shame . . . for you, anyway. He's such a nice guy, and he really seemed to care about you."

"He did . . . he does. Actually we're on pretty good terms. I like him better as a friend than a boyfriend."

Mary leaned forward and cupped her chin in her hands. "I'm sure other men are pursuing you. Anyone interesting?"

I nearly squirmed. "Well, I've been dating David Wentworth for a while now."

Mary took a small sip of iced tea. "Of course, David Wentworth. How's it going?"

"Pretty well. We enjoy . . . each other's company." I could talk to Mary about nearly anything, but I was sure she'd be shocked if she knew what I did with David.

"I see." She gave me a penetrating gaze, and I knew that she knew. She knew that David and I had a wild sex life—and that sex was the primary focus of our relationship.

"Are you falling in love with him?" she asked casually.

"Oh, no, it's not like that," I responded rapidly. "Really, it's just a fling. We don't have much in common. Like I said, we just . . . enjoy each other. It's not going to last long. Actually, I'm surprised it's lasted as long as it has."

"I see," she said again. "Well, sometimes it's fun to have a little fling. I'm glad you're having a good time." Mary was a talented actress, but I knew her too well. She was worried about me.

I leaned across the table and touched her hand. "It's okay, Mary. I remember what you said about being careful with David. He's not going to hurt me. I won't let him."

As I walked along Central Park West to a bus stop, I thought about our conversation. I had told Mary the truth about David—it was just a fling. I wasn't falling in love with him.

"But you could fall in love with him," said Miss Prudence. *"If he'd let you."*

"He'll never let me. He's so careful to keep his distance," I replied.

It was a thought I'd kept at the back of my mind. The truth had been nagging at me, but I'd refused to acknowledge it before. David didn't want a relationship with me. He just wanted to fuck me.

"He's been using you," Miss Prudence pointed out. *"You're just his little sex toy. He'll dump you when he's had enough."*

I felt a sudden dull ache in my stomach. I sat down on a bench and stared at autumn leaves falling from the Central Park trees. Had I been fooling myself all this time, pretending this affair with David was wonderful when I was just allowing myself to be used?

Miss Hornypants butted in. *"You enjoy the sex as much as he does. So who's being used? You knew from the start this wouldn't last. You and David aren't right for each other. A serious relationship would never work."*

I closed my eyes and expelled a long breath. Miss H. was right again. David and I had nothing in common except sex. So I'd just keep enjoying our time together. When it ended, I'd move on to a real relationship.

The ache in my stomach was gone. I decided to skip the bus

and walk the rest of the way home. I was going to enjoy this glorious fall day. I was going to savor every moment fully and not fret about the future.

I found this resolution was difficult to keep. I couldn't help feeling aware of the shallow nature of my relationship with David. We fucked. Then we fucked some more. That was it. Even our conversations revolved around sex.

My attempts at real dialogue failed miserably. One night at Francesca's I made the mistake of bringing up his ex-wife, Anna.

"So how long were you married?" I asked.

"Three years." He seemed very intent on cutting his filet mignon.

"If you don't mind my asking . . . what happened? Why did you split up?"

David glanced up from his plate briefly. "She was an alcoholic. I used to find empty gin bottles hidden in shoe boxes. I tried to persuade her to get help, but she refused."

"Oh . . . I'm so sorry."

David shrugged. "The last straw was when she started talking about having a baby. I knew she'd keep drinking throughout her pregnancy . . . with God knows what kind of results. So I gave her an ultimatum—rehab or divorce. She chose divorce."

"God, that must have been rough. Did she ever go to rehab? Is she okay these days?"

David shrugged again. "Beats me. I wanted her out of my life as quickly as possible, so I gave her a large one-time settlement. We haven't talked since the last meeting at our attorney's office. I heard that she moved to California."

I was shocked by his dismissive tone. I was sure he was just covering up his pain and disappointment. "It must have been so hard for you to end your marriage that way—"

"Gillian," he interrupted brusquely. "I don't like to talk about Anna. Let's drop the subject."

"Of course." We were silent for a few minutes. I gave him a tentative smile and leaned forward. "I have a fantasy that I think will interest you," I whispered. "Would you like me to tell you about it?"

"God, yes." He caressed my cheek. "Tell me everything, Gillian. Tell me what you'd like me to do to you."

I leaned closer and breathed softly into his ear. "First I want you to strip me—very slowly—in front of your dressing-room mirror. Take off everything except my panties. Then stand behind me and fondle my breasts. Rub your hard-on against my ass. . . ."

"And then?"

"And then stroke my pussy through my panties. You know how that makes me so wet. . . ."

We were back in our comfort zone—madly in lust. As soon as we arrived at his apartment, David dragged me by the hand to his dressing room. He followed the details of my fantasy exactly—slowly unbuttoning my blouse, unhooking my bra, unzipping my skirt. Each piece of clothing fell to the floor until I was standing in my panties and high heels. I faced the mirror and watched as he stood behind me and gently squeezed my breasts. My nipples immediately stiffened. I felt his hard cock rubbing against my ass. He left one hand on my breasts and slid the other hand slowly down my body until he reached my panties. He stroked my pussy through the silk of my panties until I moaned. I was dripping wet; my juice soaked the crotch of the panties.

He stopped for a moment, making me sigh with frustration. He unzipped his fly and pulled out his cock. "Gillian . . . I want you to spread your cheeks for me. Don't worry, I won't hurt you."

I spread my cheeks and felt the swollen head of his cock rubbing against my hole. David slid his hand under the elastic of my panties and massaged my clit until I whimpered. I came very intensely, ripples of pleasure running through my body. He pressed the head of his cock harder against my asshole; I heard his deep groan as I felt the warm gush of cum between my cheeks.

7

Anita and I went home to Hanover for Thanksgiving. David had gone to Denver to be with his parents.

Mom and Dad and my sister, Caroline, were disappointed to hear that Steve and I had broken up. I was vague about the reason—they were a little more provincial than Aunt Mary. Steve's closet homosexuality would have shocked them.

I was also vague when they asked about new developments in my love life. "Oh, I'm just dating casually," I responded. I suspected that my parents wouldn't approve of David—a considerably older, divorced man was not a good match for their little girl. Caroline would have been thrilled to hear that I was dating a super-rich near-celebrity—but she would speculate about engagement rings and wedding dates. Caroline was a high school senior who lived for romance. She worked part time at a bridal boutique and aspired to become a bridal consultant. Her romantic mind would have been baffled by the intensely sexual nature of my relationship with David.

After Thanksgiving dinner we all gathered in the living room to watch *The Wizard of Oz* on DVD. It was only nine o'clock, but I was half asleep. Every time I returned to Hanover I seemed to immediately lose my metropolitan sophistication. As I struggled to keep my eyelids open, I wondered how I managed to stay up so late in New York.

My cell phone rang, startling me out of my stupor. "Hello," I mumbled.

"Hi, it's me."

"David!" I yelped. Raised eyebrows and curious glances from Dad, Mom and Caroline.

"Excuse me," I mumbled and went out to the porch to take the call. The cold night air and the stimulation of David's voice gave me a rush of energy.

"I'm so glad you called," I gushed to David. "I love spending time with my family, but things get a little dull around here."

"Same here. Two days with my parents and I'm itching to get back to New York. And back to you."

I felt a little thrill. "So you miss me?"

"Yes. Especially certain parts of you."

I wavered between feeling insulted and feeling gratified. I decided to take his comment as a joke.

"Oh, I miss certain parts of you, too. Especially a certain long, hard part."

"Gillian, are you alone?"

"Yes."

"Good. I want you to play with yourself."

"Wait a sec." I glanced around. It was pitch dark on the porch. I scrunched into a corner far from the door and windows.

"Okay," I whispered. "I'm unzipping the fly of my jeans. Tell me what you want me to do."

"I want you to slide your hand into your panties and rub your clit."

I obeyed and felt tingling warmth radiate slowly through my body. "What are you doing, David?"

"You know what you do to me, Gillian. Just your voice turns me on . . . makes me so hard. I'm stroking my cock and thinking about your sexy little body. I'm fantasizing about licking your clit until you scream."

"Yes, I love the way you lick me. Your tongue feels so good. . . ."

"Slide your fingers inside your pussy, Gillian. Think about my cock."

I slid two fingers inside my tight, slippery opening. "David . . . do you love to fuck me?"

His breathing was harsh. "Yes."

"Say it. Say it until I come."

"I love to fuck you, Gillian. I love to fuck you . . ."

I heard his deep moan as he came—so familiar now but still so exciting. I nearly bit through my lower lip as my muscles convulsed around my fingers. I was becoming an expert at suppressing my orgasmic cries. Too bad there wasn't much call for this skill in my acting career.

"That was . . . fabulous," I gasped.

"Yes, it was." His breathing slowed and evened. "I'll be back in New York next Monday. I'll call you then, Gillian. Good night."

"Good night, David." Once again I felt disappointed by his abrupt manner. And once again I shrugged off the feeling.

When I returned to the living room all eyes turned to me again. "Who's David?" Mom asked, trying to sound casual.

I wiped beads of sweat from my upper lip. "Oh, just an old friend. I hadn't heard from him in a while, so I was surprised when he called."

Caroline stared at my flushed face. "Really? Just an old friend?" She gave me her *I don't believe you* look

"Yes, Caroline, he's just an old friend," I responded with my harshest *drop the subject now* glare. No one mentioned David or the phone call again.

* * *

The day after Thanksgiving was brilliant and crisp. Anita called and suggested climbing Mt. Monadnock. I groaned at the thought of the strenuous hike.

"Come on, we haven't done that hike in years. It'll be good for us. We can bring a delicious picnic lunch from Goldie's Deli. We'll earn the right to eat pastrami and chocolate chip cookies," she coaxed.

The thought of Goldie's pastrami and cookies persuaded me. I met Anita in the parking lot at the base of the mountain. She looked like a panther in black jeans and a black turtleneck. She started striding up the mountain as I stumbled after her. A third of the way up the trail I was panting and sweating. "Anita, I've got to stop and rest," I gasped. "Christ, I'm out of shape. I've lost a few pounds, but I've got to start hitting the gym again."

Anita wasn't even breathing hard. "Come on, Monroe," she barked in her best imitation of Ms. Cantwell, our sadistic junior high gym teacher. "Get your ass in gear."

"Use the carrot, not the stick," I panted.

"Okay. Pa-*strami*, *cook*-ies, pa-*strami*, *cook*-ies," she chanted. It worked. I staggered after her up the trail.

The hard labor was worth it. The view from the summit was more spectacular than I'd remembered—wave upon wave of bright foliage spread far below us. The air was so sharp and fresh I could almost taste the purity.

We scarfed down the sandwiches, chips, dill pickles and cookies in five minutes flat.

Anita belched delicately and sighed happily. "I haven't had a meal like that since . . . god, since I started modeling." She stretched out on a warm, flat rock, looking like a very content feline. "I thought I'd never say this, but sometimes I really miss Hanover. I get so sick of New York and modeling. One day I'm going to move back here. I'm going to hike and bike and camp and eat lunch at Goldie's every day."

"When did you become a Girl Scout? Just a few years ago you couldn't wait to get out of here."

She opened her eyes and squinted in the bright sunlight. "I know. But things have changed. I've had enough of the glamour"—she put air quotes around the word—"of big-city living and the fashion industry."

I pulled off my hiking boots and socks to massage my sore feet. "I can't imagine moving back here. Well, a weekend cottage would be nice. Now that my career is finally going somewhere, I'm happier than ever in New York."

"Is your love life okay, too? How is Mr. Fantastic Stud these days?"

"Oh, it's going pretty well. Little things aggravate me. Like I always get his voice mail when I call his cell—but he always calls me back quickly. And I wish we could do more things together. But I've pretty much accepted that this is just a fling, an affair, a prolonged sexual encounter, whatever you want to call it."

Anita rolled over on to her stomach. "Hey, sometimes lust turns into love."

"I doubt it, in this case. But I have to confess that it's fun to date a really rich guy. Wealth has never been one of my criteria for dating a guy, but I'm definitely enjoying David's money." I pulled on my socks and laced up my boots.

Anita stood and stretched. "When am I going to meet the Amazing Cockmaster, anyway?"

"Oh, sometime soon. We'll have to plan it," I said vaguely. Actually, I'd avoided this topic. When men met Anita for the first time, they almost always reacted with slack-jawed wonder. I couldn't stand the idea of David being attracted to my gorgeous best friend.

I heaved my tired body up and brushed leaves off my butt. "Come on, we should head back down before it starts to get dark."

As we hiked down the mountain, I remembered that I hadn't told Anita about David's call the previous night. I wondered why I was being secretive about him—first with my family, and now with my best friend.

8

David called me as soon as we were both back in New York. We had a few days of incredible, nearly nonstop sex. I especially liked it when he teased me, playing with my tits and pussy and ass until I couldn't bear it any longer. I'd beg him for his cock, and he'd fuck me hard, shooting cum deep into my pussy or between my cheeks or into my mouth or all over my breasts.

The sex seemed more intense and satisfying every time we went to bed. And then suddenly everything nearly fell apart.

I was lying in the four-poster bed one morning, ogling David's hard body as he dressed for work. He casually mentioned that he had to go to Boston to work on the condo project.

"For how long?" I stretched lazily.

"Not sure. At least a week." He sat on the bed to put on his shoes.

I gave him what I hoped was my most charming smile. "You know, I don't have anything going on this week. No auditions, no temp jobs. I could come with you. I haven't been to Boston in ages."

He glanced away from me, intent on fastening his watch

strap. I hated it when he avoided my gaze. I knew it meant he was going to say something I wouldn't like.

"Sorry, Gillian. It's not a good idea. I'm going to be working twelve-hour days."

"Well, that's no big deal. I know Boston well. When I was a kid, my family used to go there all the time. I can keep myself occupied while you're working. We'll still have the nights . . . and the mornings . . . to have fun." I lightly massaged the back of his neck.

He shrugged my hand away. "Sorry, Gillian."

I felt insulted—and furious. "Jesus Christ, David, what is wrong with you? Why don't you want to do anything with me except fuck? Am I so boring out of bed?"

His intense blue eyes flashed. "Back off, Gillian. Don't make demands of me." There was a sharp edge in his voice I'd never heard before.

I flung the bedcovers aside and started yanking on my clothes. "I haven't made any demands at all. But I'm getting a little sick of being treated like a call girl."

"I don't think a call girl would enjoy fucking me as much as you do," David snapped.

Tears of rage pricked at my eyes. I started toward the door. "Let me know when you're ready to have a real conversation about our relationship," I snarled.

As I turned to go, he grabbed my arm. "Look, I'm sorry. Okay? I'm *sorry*."

I studied his face. His expression was tense; he still looked more angry than contrite. But I knew he was someone who found it difficult to apologize.

"Okay. I'm sorry, too," I whispered. "It's just that we spend all our time in bed. Sometimes I want to do something different . . . have some fun with you."

The tension eased from his face. He sat back down on the bed and pulled me onto his lap. "I understand. I promise we'll do something fun when I get back from Boston. Let me know what you'd like to do, and I'll arrange it. Anything you want, Gillian." He softly stroked my hair.

I felt a burst of happiness. Maybe David did have some feelings for me after all. "I'd like that. I'd like that a lot."

"Good," he murmured. "I'm thinking of going to Bermuda in March for a few days to look at some investment properties. Perhaps you can come with me."

"Oh, I'd love that," I squeaked. "Maybe we should fight more often. Making up is so much fun."

He laughed. "You do make me feel good, Gillian. And not just in bed."

Another brief moment of triumph.

David was gone for ten days. I resisted the temptation to call his cell. "Smart move," Anita said approvingly. "Be a little cool and distant. Make him miss you."

David called only once, late at night. We had mind-blowing phone sex again—it was clearly one of his favorite pastimes. One of mine, too.

"You have such a dirty little mind, Gillian," he whispered into the phone. "The way you talk about sex . . . your voice makes my cock so hard."

I squirmed with delight."Yes . . . I love to make you very hard and excited. And I love to make you come hard. I'm wearing only a T-shirt and lace panties. Do you want me to play with myself?"

"Yes, darling. Put your hand down your panties and play with your pussy."

I slid my hand under the lace and rubbed my clit until I was dripping. "David—imagine me tied up in your four-poster bed. Spread eagle."

He responded with a deep moan. "I love that idea, Gillian . . . tell me more."

"My wrists and my ankles are tied. My legs are spread wide so my pussy is completely exposed. My nipples are hard, and I'm breathing very fast. I'm wet and excited and completely helpless." I paused.

"Don't stop, Gillian, please don't stop—"

"You play with my tits, my pussy and my ass. You make me wait a long time before you let me come. Then you straddle my face so I can suck the head of your cock and lick your tight balls. You finally return to my pussy—you stroke it and lick it until I'm begging for your cock. Then you fuck me long and hard until I scream. How do you come, David? Tell me how you come."

"I pull out my cock and spurt all over your beautiful tits. Oh, god, Gillian—"

I rubbed my clit harder and faster; David's orgasmic cry was enough to push me over the edge. Pleasure exploded through my body.

When David returned to New York he kept his promise to do something fun together. I told him I wanted to see *Spamalot*. He managed to get superb seats, I didn't ask how, but I assumed it involved paying a lot of money. We laughed our heads off during the play. For the first time I actually felt close to him.

He held my hand during the drive home. "Have you ever done musical comedy, Gillian? You'd be great in a play like *Spamalot.*"

"Afraid not. I can't sing to save my life. I sound like a hyena with laryngitis."

He grinned. "You have other talents, darling." He unbuttoned the top of my coat and slipped his hand in to fondle my hard nipples. The sexual tension had been escalating all evening. We'd been apart for nearly two weeks and had just spent three hours in close proximity.

In the elevator he pressed me against the back wall and kissed me hungrily as I rubbed the hard bulge between his legs. When we stepped into the foyer he tore off my coat, blouse and bra. "Turn around and spread your legs," he ordered. He lifted my skirt and bent me over the foyer table. He yanked my panties down; I moaned as he massaged my clit and lips with his thumb. I heard him breathing hard as he fumbled with his belt and zipper. He thrust his cock deep into my warm, wet pussy, making me whimper with pleasure. I could feel his balls rubbing against my lips; the sensation was exquisite. He pressed the palm of his hand against my mound. I came with the third thrust; he exploded with the fourth.

Later that night we acted out my phone-sex fantasy. David tied me up with silk neckties and teased me until I came repeatedly. In the morning I woke up to find his hand between my thighs, coaxing me into a frenzy again.

"I can't get enough of you, Gillian," he panted.

"And I can't get enough of you." I pulled his cock into me and wrapped my legs around him. At that moment I wanted the affair to last forever.

That morning Al dropped David off at his office and then drove me to my apartment. I loved chatting with Al. He was a huge teddy bear of a guy with a thick Jersey accent—a very benign version of Tony Soprano.

I asked him how long he'd worked for David. "Eight years. Mr. Wentworth is the nicest employer I've ever had. He's always thoughtful, not like some of these rat bastards who treat drivers like slaves. He's generous, too, helping me put my kid Kevin through college."

"That is nice," I replied. I secretly wondered if Al felt obligated to talk David up to me.

He pulled over in front of my building. I thanked him as I opened the door.

"You're welcome, Miranda," he said cheerfully.

I froze and stared at him. "My name is Gillian."

He slapped his forehead. "Where's my brain today? I was thinking about my cousin Miranda this morning. Sorry, Gillian!"

"No problem. Thanks again, Al."

It was a minor incident, but it nagged at me. I wondered if Al had been driving a Miranda around—or if he couldn't remember my name because he had driven so many of David's women around.

"*Stop speculating and creating problems,*" Miss Prudence scolded. "*Get into your workout clothes and get to the gym.*"

For once I followed Miss P.'s advice.

Christmas was only a few weeks away. I fretted constantly about what to get for David. "How do you shop for a man who has everything and can buy everything?" I moaned to Anita one afternoon at Java Java.

"I'll help you figure it out. There must be something unique we can find for him."

We pondered the problem for a while, but even double espressos didn't jolt our brains enough to provide a solution.

"How about a really nice Italian silk necktie?" Anita suggested.

"He already has a couple hundred." I blushed a little when I thought about my intimate acquaintance with some of those ties.

"Oh. Scratch that idea," said Anita.

A few minutes later she nearly shouted, "Got it! Sexy boudoir pictures. I know a great photographer who'd take some shots of you for a reduced rate."

"I don't know," I said dubiously. "David would probably like the photos, but I'm not really comfortable with that. I guess I'll just have to wait for inspiration to hit me."

Fortunately inspiration did strike a few days later. I noticed a new history of the Civil War in a bookstore window. A little light went off in my head. On our first date David had told me he was a huge Civil War buff—he had ancestors who fought on both sides. I went into the store and perused the book. It was perfect, an exhaustive history filled with fascinating photos, illustrations and maps. It had just been published, so David probably didn't have it yet.

I cringed when I looked at the price—nearly $100. I bit the bullet and paid it. I figured David would probably spend a small fortune on my present. As I walked home with my purchase I felt so relieved—and pleased at the thought of David's reaction when he opened my gift.

David called me a few days before Christmas and asked me if I'd like to come over. I pretended to be uncertain. "Depends . . . are you going to ravish me?" I asked.

"Of course. I want to ravish you every time I look at you."

"Oh, goody. I'll be there at seven."

I carefully wrapped the book in peacock-blue paper and gold ribbon. It looked magnificent. Again I felt relieved and gratified that I'd found the perfect gift.

David kissed me passionately as soon as I stepped into the foyer. As I reached up to wrap my arms around his neck, my tote bag fell to the floor with a *thunk*.

"What's that?" he asked.

"Oh, just something I wanted to show you later." My hands glided down to his ass. "We have more important things to do right now. Slide your hands up my skirt and touch my pussy. . . . Make me wet. . . ."

He played with my pussy until I was just on the brink of orgasm. "Do you want to come, Gillian?" he whispered.

"Yes, please let me come."

He yanked my panties down and spread my lips.

"Do you want me to lick your pussy?"

"Yes, please lick my pussy."

"I want you to scream."

"Yes, I'll scream . . . please let me come."

He fell to his knees and buried his tongue between my lips. The sensation was unbearable, so good I couldn't stand it. I screamed as my body was racked by orgasmic waves. David stood and smiled at me, pleased by the pleasure he had given me.

"How do you want to fuck me? How do you want to come?" I gasped.

"I want to fuck your mouth and come all over your breasts."

I pulled off my sweater and sat on the couch with my legs spread wide so he could look at my wet pussy while I sucked his cock. He thrust the shaft between my lips for a long time. He stopped for a moment. "Here I come, darling," he panted.

I clutched his ass as he pumped harder. He suddenly pulled the shaft out, and I watched the cum shoot out of the head, sweet warm stickiness dripping all over my breasts.

After another long, sweaty session on the floor in front of his dressing-room mirror, we decided to take a dinner break. He had Chinese food delivered—the best I'd ever tasted. We ate at the enormous smoked-glass dining table, laughing at our pathetic efforts to use chopsticks. Most of the kung pao shrimp and ginger chicken ended up on the glass table. David dismissed my efforts to clean up. "The housekeeper will do it. As you said before, we have better things to do. . . ."

"Wait a sec. There's something I want to do first." I retrieved my tote bag and pulled out the bright, shiny package. "Here, this is for you." I kissed his cheek as I handed him the gift.

He looked uncomfortable. "Gillian, you didn't have to—"

"Open it, open it!" I bounced up and down on my chair like an overexcited toddler.

He slowly tore away the wrapping. "Wow, this is great. You

remembered that I'm a Civil War buff. I haven't even heard of this book. . . . It looks amazing. Thanks."

"You're welcome. I'm so glad you like it. You're not an easy person to shop for." I leaned over to give him another kiss.

He gave me an embarrassed look. "Um, Gillian, I'm really sorry, but I didn't get anything for you. I meant to, but I've been so busy lately—"

"I see," I said coldly. I was in shock. He didn't have *time*? What a lame excuse. He could have told one of his minions to get a gift for me. He could have given me a Christmas card, for God's sake.

I stood up. "I'm leaving now," I said stiffly. I picked up my tote bag and headed for the foyer.

David trailed after me. "Gillian, please don't leave—"

"Please get my coat." I felt and sounded half dead. I pressed the elevator button.

He opened the hall closet door. "Wait a minute." He pulled his own coat out of the closet and took his wallet from the inside pocket. He removed five crisp hundred-dollar bills and held them out to me.

I slapped them to the floor. "What the hell do you think I am? Some kind of hooker?" I screeched.

"Of course not. I just want you to buy something for yourself. Something really nice—"

I reached into the closet and jerked my coat from its hanger. "No, thanks. I don't want to see you again." I turned my back on him as the elevator doors slid open.

"Gillian, please don't be upset. I'll make it up to you—"

I didn't respond. I stepped into the elevator and looked down at the floor. I pressed the lobby button, and the doors closed.

As the elevator descended I had to fight back the tears. I declined politely when the doorman offered to get me a cab. Half a block from David's building I burst into tears.

I ended up walking all the way home. It took me over an hour. I was so upset I was oblivious to the howling winter wind and the pedestrians who turned to stare at my tear-stained face.

I can't believe it, I just can't believe it, I kept saying to myself. *Can't believe our magical evening turned to shit. Can't believe I bought that wonderful gift for an asshole. Can't believe he didn't get me anything. Can't believe it ended this way.*

9

I returned to Hanover for Christmas. Anita had planned to stay in New York, but when I told her about my disastrous evening and breakup with David, she decided to come with me. I was so glad to get out of the city—and to have my sympathetic friend with me.

We spent a lot of time trudging through the snowy woods. During our rambles she listened patiently while I ranted about David. "We'd been sleeping together for four months and he didn't even get me a fucking *card.* It just shows how little he thinks of me. And then to offer me money—that was the final insult."

Anita glanced at me from under her long, dark lashes. "You know, I've been thinking about that. The money part, I mean."

I stopped and stared at her. "You don't think I should have accepted a wad of cash, do you?"

"No . . . but I wonder if he was trying to make you a tentative offer. You said several times that it was just a sexual thing. That's what it was to him, anyway. I think maybe he wanted you to be his mistress."

I gawked at her. "Mistress? You mean like a kept woman?"

"Yep. It's pretty common with these super-rich guys. They have wives—women who are appropriate for their lifestyles—and lovers on the side."

"David isn't married. He's divorced."

"But he's going to remarry one of these days. A guy like David needs a wife. And, no offense, Gillian, but you're not the right person to fill the position of Mrs. Wentworth. He needs someone older who shares more of his interests. Golf, country clubs, social climbing—all that shit."

I sank down on a granite boulder. "Well, I guess that's true. But if he wanted a purely sexual thing with no complications, why didn't he use a fancy escort service? I've heard that some of those girls are very beautiful—and very skilled."

Anita sat next to me and looked me in the eyes. "David didn't want a high-priced call girl. He wanted *you*. And when he tried to give you that cash, he may have been testing the waters."

I shifted uncomfortably on the cold rock. "You could be right."

"So if he calls you and suggests this arrangement, how will you respond?"

"God, I don't know. My initial feeling is that I'd turn him down. But the truth is I miss him, Anita. I was so angry that night I never expected to miss him at all. But I do."

"Well, there would be some advantages to being his mistress. You'd know exactly where you stood with him. You could make each other happy for a while. He'd probably give you some kind of allowance, which would give you some financial security. And David is hot. It's not like you'd be having sex with some repulsive rich guy like"—she shuddered—"Donald Trump or Bill Gates."

I laughed for the first time in days. "This is true. And some extra money would be welcome. My bank balance is healthy at the moment, but there are so many dry periods when I'm earning nothing at all."

"Well, you should think about this. I wouldn't be surprised at all if David called and made you an offer."

I thought about it hard, and it didn't take me long to make a decision. It was a tempting idea—I was so tired of struggling for so long. My brief periods of affluence were overshadowed by long droughts of poverty. David had more money than he could ever spend. And what else did he have to offer me, anyway? Certainly not a relationship.

But I just couldn't do it. It didn't seem right, the very idea made me feel icky. I certainly wouldn't feel comfortable in the position of mistress if David remarried. And, most importantly, I wanted a *real* boyfriend, a *real* relationship. How could I possibly pursue that as another man's kept woman? I could just imagine it: "Sorry, Jeff, I can't go out with you tonight. I'm on call. David might want to have sex with me."

I sighed. *I'm probably fretting over nothing. The issue will never come up.* I'd been half expecting—with hope and apprehension—that David would call. But my cell phone was silent.

My parents and my sister noticed my moodiness and preoccupation. "I think Gillian is in love," teased Caroline as we trimmed the Christmas tree.

"Oh, just shut up, Caroline," I snapped. My sister looked wounded.

"*Gillian!*" my mother thundered.

"Sorry," I muttered. "I've been stressed out lately."

"It's Christmas, for Christ's sake. We're supposed to be enjoying ourselves and sharing quality family time, damnit." My mother took holidays very seriously.

"Sorry, Mom. Sorry, Caroline," I apologized meekly.

I summoned all my acting talent, and for the rest of my stay

I played the part of Happy, Carefree Gillian. But at night I felt so alone in my bed. Instead of stifling my cries of ecstasy, I had to suppress the sound of my weeping.

I was glad to return to New York and real acting. But even that was problematic. The shoot for the second radio-station commercial was so difficult compared to the first time around. Joe, the director, was exasperated with me.

"What the hell is wrong with you, Gillian? You're supposed to be happy, happy, happy about this great radio station. You look and sound like your puppy, your kitten and your grandma all just died."

"Sorry, Joe." I was apologizing to everyone these days. "Can we try it again after a short break?"

"Okay. Ten minutes. I expect cheerful and peppy and cute when you come back."

I sat in the ladies' room with my head in my hands. I had been so happy about David during the first radio commercial shoot. Now I just felt bleak.

Suck it up, Gillian, I told myself. *You can't spend the rest of your life feeling this way*. I took a long, deep breath and cleared my mind—a brief form of meditation.

During the next take Joe was pleased by my extreme perkiness. "That's it, Gillian! That's just what we needed. Great job."

Okay. So I was at least partially back on track. Now I just needed to get the rest of my life together.

Steve and Oliver invited me to a New Year's Eve party; they included Anita in the invitation. I was so depressed I didn't want to go, but Anita insisted. She had broken up with Michael for the zillionth time—and she insisted it was over for good. "Both of us need to meet new guys," she declared.

We both glammed up for the occasion. Anita wore her

Versace miniskirt with a gold sequined bustier. I wore the black lace blouse with a short black skirt and high black boots. The effort was mostly wasted—nearly all the other guests were gay males—but at least they appreciated our fashion sense.

Steve and I sat on bar stools at his kitchen island and chatted. He looked happier than I'd ever seen him. I asked him how his coming out had gone over with his conservative parents. "Oh, they were horrified and appalled, of course, but I think they're starting to come around. They haven't disowned me, at any rate."

Oliver had already moved in with him. *A few months together and they're already committed,* I thought gloomily. Steve asked about David; I said we weren't seeing each other anymore and quickly changed the subject.

Anita and I left soon after midnight. The cab driver dropped me off first. Before I exited the cab, Anita gave me a big hug. "This new year will be great for both of us, I just know it," she said.

I gave her a sad smile. "I certainly hope you're right about that. I don't see how things could get much worse."

I woke up late the next morning and immediately thought, *No David. Not today or any other day. Happy New Year, Gillian.*

I made myself some strong coffee and took a hot shower. It had snowed a little the night before, and the sun was dazzling on the fresh white frosting. Manhattan looked magical. I decided to go for a long, solitary walk to get my head together. I had put on my coat and was hunting for my keys when my cell rang.

"Hello?"

"Don't hang up, Gillian."

David. I felt my heart plummet. "What is it?" I asked coldly.

"Look, I'm so sorry about what happened that night. I really did mean to get you a present, but the time just slipped by. And of course I shouldn't have offered you cash, but you were so upset and I wanted to fix it somehow. . . ."

I was silent. David had caught me completely off guard. I didn't know how to respond.

"I think about you constantly, Gillian. I want to have sex with you all the time. That last time with you . . . it was the best sex I've ever had. Please say you'll see me again."

So it was still all about sex. I remained silent.

"I have a Christmas present for you. I think you'll really like it." His tone was wheedling.

I finally spoke. "I just don't think it can work with us, David. We obviously have different expectations."

"We can talk about that. Just say you'll see me again. *Please*."

I hesitated and then finally relented. "Okay. We'll talk."

"Great. Can I come by to pick you up in twenty minutes?"

"All right." My voice was faint, but I couldn't help feeling a small surge of joy.

I felt a sense of déjà vu as I slid across the leather seat of the Mercedes. I sat as far away from David as possible. "Hi, Al, how are you?" I asked stiffly.

Al glanced around from the front seat. "Fine, thanks. Happy New Year," he replied.

"Gillian. . . ." I felt the touch of David's hand on my cheek. I was forced to look at him. "You look wonderful," he said.

"Thanks," I said cooly. "You look great, too."

He did. Why did I ever think this man was merely attractive? He was devastating; he had more presence and charisma than a thousand pretty boys. He smiled tentatively at me, and I experienced the familiar feeling of jellied knees.

The Mercedes was heading uptown. "Where are we going?" I asked. I had assumed David would take me somewhere for a drink or a cup of coffee so we could talk in relative privacy.

"It's a surprise. I'm taking you to your Christmas present," David said. He reached over and covered my hand with his, giving it a gentle squeeze. I considered pulling it away, but somehow I couldn't summon up the strength.

Al pulled over in front of a brownstone on West Seventy-Third Street. David helped me alight from the car. "My present is here?" I asked, feeling confused.

"Yes, it's inside. I bought this building a few months ago, and I wanted to show it to you." He escorted me up the front steps and into the lobby.

"Very nice," I murmured. It looked like a Victorian that had recently been renovated.

"Thanks. We spent a lot of time and money restoring this building. I think all the effort was worth it. Let me show you one of the apartments."

We went up another flight of stairs to the second-story front unit. He opened the door and stood aside to let me in.

It was beautiful. High ceilings, exquisite moulding, polished wood floors, floods of light coming through the large windows. Just one bedroom, but it was enormous. The bathroom was nearly as big as my entire apartment. Two walk-in closets. A modern kitchen that could have been featured on any home-makeover show.

I offered appropriate compliments. I was still puzzled—why were we here?

David answered my question. "If you want it, it's yours."

I didn't understand at first. "This apartment? I can't afford it, David."

"I'll charge you only four hundred dollars a month."

I felt a little dizzy. I was currently paying twice as much for my tiny rat hole. I didn't know how to respond.

"Gillian, please let me do this for you. I'd really like you to take the apartment. If you don't, I'll just rent it to someone else for four times as much." His voice had a pleading note I'd never heard before.

"I just don't know, David. Can I think about it? I promise I'll let you know my decision as soon as possible."

He looked relieved. "Okay, that's fine. I have another present for you, Gillian. Look in the bedroom closet."

I opened the closet door but didn't see anything in the cavernous space.

"Top shelf on the right," said David.

I found a rectangular box—pale lilac with the word VIOLETTE stamped in gold cursive script. I'd read about Violette in *Vogue*—it was a Swiss company that made exquisite and wildly expensive lingerie. This was the kind of gift I had expected.

"Open it," David urged.

I removed the top and slowly pulled aside the purple tissue paper. I thought I'd find a sexy confection of lace and silk in black or red. I was surprised when I lifted out a long nightgown of fine white cotton. Embroidered pink rosebuds were scattered over the gown. The neckline and long sleeves were trimmed with pink silk ribbons.

"Thank you. It's lovely," I said.

David stared at me with longing. I knew he wanted me—badly. And I knew I couldn't possibly resist him.

"Gillian, I'd like you to wear that nightgown for me. Now."

I couldn't say no. I didn't even hesitate. "I'll be back in a minute."

I changed in the bathroom. When I stepped back into the bedroom, David rushed at me.

"No," I said almost harshly. "You have to wait. I want this to be as slow as we can stand it."

He stepped back. I looked at the enormous bulge of his hard-on and felt a warm trickle of wetness between my thighs.

"Don't move. Just look at me," I said. The material of the nighty was so sheer my hard nipples and the dark patch of my pussy hair were clearly visible. I slowly untied the ribbons at my neck and slid my hand in to fondle my breasts.

"Gillian. . . ." David's voice was strained.

I slid my hand down and rubbed my pussy through the fine cotton. I watched David's face as beads of sweat broke out on his forehead.

"Your cock is so hard . . . I want to suck it."

"Yes, please suck it for me, Gillian."

I sank to my knees and teased him by rubbing the bulge through his pants. Then I unzipped his fly as slowly as possible and drew out his straining cock.

I teased him again with my flickering tongue—over the head and shaft and then around his balls. He was breathing so hard I thought he might hyperventilate.

I slid the shaft all the way into my mouth until his balls were pressing against my chin. I remained still for a few minutes. His breathing became more ragged. He finally said, "I can't stand it," and pulled out his cock. "I need to touch you, Gillian." He helped me to my feet and crushed my mouth with his. His warm fingers invaded the bodice and caressed my breasts. Then he slowly lifted the nightie up to my waist and explored my pussy and ass. He used one index finger to gently rub my clit while he rubbed my pussy lips together with his other hand. I held on to his shoulders, writhing under his touch, digging in my nails as waves of pleasure flooded through me. I cried out loud like an animal in heat.

"That's my girl . . . that's my sweet, sexy girl," David murmured as I came. I fell against his chest, completely limp. He took my hand and pulled me into the kitchen. I felt like a rag doll. He lifted me up on the kitchen counter and nearly tore the exquisite nightie as he yanked it up. I spread my legs for him, exposing my wet pussy.

He thrust into me immediately. He fucked me hard, not seeming to care whether he was giving me pleasure or pain. I felt another deeply intense orgasm building. He spurted into my pussy, and at the same moment I screamed again.

It was so good, so good—I had nearly forgotten how good.

* * *

David and I sat on the bare bedroom floor with our backs pressed against the wall. His arm was around me; I rested my head against his chest.

He stroked my hair. "So will you accept my presents?"

I gave a contented sigh. "Yes. It's very generous of you, David. I do appreciate it."

"Good. I'm glad I've made you happy." He gave my left breast a gentle tweak.

"There's just one problem. I still have three months left on my lease. My landlord is a bastard—I'm sure he'll make trouble for me."

"Don't worry about it. My company will take care of it."

"But—"

"Shhh. Don't fret. You can move in here tomorrow, if you like."

"Okay. Thanks." I shifted uncomfortably on the hardwood floor. "There's something else we need to discuss. Our relationship. Our expectations."

"Yes." His voice was a little cooler, a little stiffer. "Look, Gillian, you know I can't offer you a serious relationship. We're not right for each other."

I drew away from him. "Don't you have even a little affection for me?"

He pulled me back into his embrace. "Of course I do. Look—this is what I can offer you: lots of fun. Lots of great sex. Some nice presents. An occasional trip. That's all. But we've enjoyed each other in the past, and I think we can enjoy each other for quite a while longer."

I was silent. I had been expecting this. It was the most he could offer me. But was it enough to make me happy?

"Okay," I said slowly. "We'll keep seeing each other on those terms. But you have to remember that I want a serious relationship. I'm going to keep looking for that. And if I meet a guy I really like—a guy I want to sleep with—then it has to end between us."

"That's only fair," David conceded.

"Okay. If I decide to end it, you can't make a fuss. And if you decide to end it, I won't make a fuss either. When it's over, it's over."

"It's a deal. Gillian, I'm so glad we worked this out. We may not be soul mates, but we're obviously sex mates. It's a rare thing—let's just enjoy it."

Just enjoy it—what I had told myself so many times. Perhaps I'd finally be able to do that. I smiled at David and leaned in to accept his kiss.

10

Anita wasn't at all surprised when I told her about my reconciliation with David. "I knew he'd keep apologizing until you forgave him," she said. "That apartment sounds like a very nice make-up gift. I wish Michael would give me presents like that. After a fight, I'm lucky to get a single wilted rose."

I chewed my thumbnail. "I still feel a little weird about accepting the apartment. It does smack of being kept."

"No, it doesn't," Anita disagreed firmly. "David said if you didn't take it he'd rent it to someone else for a lot more money. He's just doing you a favor."

"I guess. Well, I can't change my mind now anyway."

I informed my landlord that I was moving immediately. He didn't give me any crap; someone from David's company must have performed a small miracle. I rented a mini truck, and Anita helped me move my belongings over the weekend.

After hauling dozens of boxes up the stairs, we flopped down on the couch to catch our breath.

"My pathetic bits and pieces look out of place in this elegant setting." I sighed. "I mean, look at this orange couch. It's like something from the set of a seventies sitcom."

Anita massaged her sore calves. "Well, you'll be saving a lot of money on rent, so you'll be able to buy some new furniture. I know a great secondhand store on Broadway. Let's check it out tomorrow."

"Sounds good."

We were both startled by a knock on the door. "Must be one of your new neighbors," said Anita. I heaved myself off the couch and looked through the peephole. "Oh, my god, it's David!" I whispered frantically to Anita. "And I look like a wreck."

"I'll stall him while you get yourself together,"Anita whispered back. "Go on—hurry."

"Thanks!" I ran into the bathroom and yanked a hairbrush through my hair. I washed my face and spritzed myself with lily-of-the-valley cologne.

I heard voices in the living room and then laughter. I felt a nervous quaver in my stomach. *Christ, is David falling for Anita already?*

I had no reason to worry. As soon as I entered the living room, David pinned me with his gaze. He seemed barely aware of Anita.

"Hi, Gillian. Glad you've moved. I know you have a lot of unpacking to do, but I thought you might like to go out to dinner. Oh, and Anita can join us," he added as an afterthought.

"Thanks for the invite, but I have a ton of stuff to do at home," said Anita. I silently thanked her. My reconciliation with David was still fragile; we needed time alone together.

Anita made a quick escape. "Isn't she pretty?" I asked David.

"Who's pretty?" David seemed distracted. "Oh, your friend. Yes, she's very pretty." He swooped me up and carried me into the bedroom, depositing me on the unmade bed.

"I want you to wear the nightie," he said as he tore off his clothes.

I raised my eyebrows. "My, you like that nightie a lot."

"Yes, it excites me."

"So I can see." I gazed at his long, hard cock. "Your wish is my command. I'll wear anything you like. Of course, you'll probably just rip it off my body."

I changed in the bathroom and then sat on the edge of the bed. David watched intently as I slowly pulled up the nightie, spread my legs and played with my clit. He knelt in front of me. "God, Gillian, I can't wait. It seems like it's been so long. . . ."

He plunged into my pussy and slowly slid the shaft in and out as he caressed my breasts through the fine, embroidered cotton.

"I love to watch your hard cock pumping in and out of my wet pussy," I gasped. "No one has ever made me come the way you do." I gripped his shoulders and tightened my muscles around his cock. He increased the tempo; I arched my back and cried out as a powerful orgasm burst through me. His face contorted with pleasure as his hot cum filled my pussy.

Half an hour later we were lying exhausted on the floor. "That nightie does seem to inspire you to new erotic heights," I said.

He grinned at the compliment. A sudden alarming thought popped into my head.

"David," I said hesitantly. "You aren't into . . . little girls, are you?"

"God, no," he said with a scowl of disgust. "I think pedophiles should be castrated and shot. Gillian, what kind of pervert do you think I am?" There was an edge of anger in his voice.

"I don't think you're a pervert. I just wondered—I mean, the nightie . . ."

"The nightie does turn me on because it makes you look sweet and adorable," he said. "It's the seduction-of-innocence fantasy. You know—like the severe librarian who seems to be a cold virgin. You take off her glasses and pull the hairpins out of her bun, and suddenly she turns into a hot femme fatale."

"I think I know what you mean. The farmer's daughter who seems so shy . . . but you get her out into the barn and she starts acting like a sex-crazed wild animal."

He smiled and fondled my ass. "Exactly. You would look awfully cute in overalls. Maybe that should be my next present for you. We could act out a farmer's daughter fantasy."

I laughed with relief. I now understood David's strong attraction to me and why he found me so exciting in bed. I did have a sweet, innocent look, and I was often very shy. This was why David wanted me and not an exotic beauty like Anita or some gorgeous trust-fund baby. His fantasy was to seduce me—over and over again.

Neither of us felt like going out for dinner, so we ordered pizza from a local Italian restaurant. It was wonderful. "I think I'm going to love this neighborhood," I said, wiping tomato sauce off my chin. "And I absolutely love this apartment. Thank you again, David."

"My pleasure. Speaking of pleasure . . ." He leaned across the table to share a deep, pepperoni-flavored kiss with me. We had another long, torrid session on the kitchen table; I was amazed it didn't collapse under the strain of our passion. I lay on my back with my knees apart while David stood and thrust into my pussy. He made me come twice before he pulled his cock out and ejaculated all over my lips and clit. I loved the sensation of warm cum on my pussy.

I was disappointed that he didn't want to spend the night. "Sorry, honey. I have to get up at the crack of dawn tomorrow, and of course all my things are at my apartment," he said as he pulled on his black leather jacket.

Don't be oversensitive, Gillian, I told myself. *Don't make a fuss.* "Sure, I understand. Good night, and sleep tight." I gave him a casual kiss at the front door.

After he left, the apartment seemed eerily quiet and empty. I tried to shrug off the feeling of loneliness. I tuned the radio to WROL, the station that was supposed to make me so happy in the commercials. I unpacked boxes as I sang along in my hideous hyena voice to the upbeat golden oldies.

The next day Anita came over to take me to the furniture store on Broadway.

"Wow, David is fabulous," she said as we examined table lamps and rugs. "Even better looking in person than he is in photos. How did it go last night?"

"Great. We're really comfortable with each other now. And, as always, the sex was absolutely incredible. I think maybe we've finally settled into something that works for both of us."

"Glad to hear it. You and David obviously have something strong between you. It might just be intense attraction, but, hey—what's wrong with that?"

"Exactly. I think what you said before was on the mark—we're not going to grow older together, but we can make each other happy for quite a while. What do you think of this throw rug? I'm not sure about the color—it reminds me of burnt eggplant—but it's very soft."

Anita stroked it with her fingertips. "Nice. Perfect for sex on the floor."

I laughed. "Then I'll definitely buy it."

I ended up spending a few hundred dollars on a couple of rugs, lamps and a beautiful cherry occasional table. It was so nice to buy things without fretting about money. Anita helped me transport the items in a taxi. When we set them up in my apartment, the difference was remarkable. "In a few months, when you've had a chance to replace everything, you'll have a really lovely home," Anita said approvingly.

"Yes . . . I want to create a cozy, warm atmosphere. God, Anita, I'm so happy here—it's so great to come home to a place I really love. I just hope my lucky streak lasts."

David and I experienced a second-honeymoon period. Everything went smoothly; the sex was as hot as ever, and we avoided any squabbles. I had told him I wanted to look for a serious relationship, but I had no interest in other men. No one seemed as exciting as David.

He usually came over to my new apartment, which was fine with me. His place was stunning, but I was never entirely comfortable there. It was too big, too sterile, too fancy . . . just too much. I felt more relaxed in my charming brownstone.

He rarely spent the night with me, which I found troubling, but I was careful not to complain. He was also careful, trying his best to keep me happy—in bed and out of bed. He often brought me small gifts—a pot of miniature red roses to brighten up my living room or an extravagant basket of goodies from a deli. One night he gave me a pink baby T with REAL . . . AND SPECTACULAR printed across the chest. I felt flattered and a little embarrassed. I was too shy to wear it in public, but he loved me to wear it in private with a pair of skimpy panties . . . and nothing else.

We had sex in every room of my apartment—even the walk-in closets. I sucked him off in the shower; he licked my pussy in front of the bedroom closet mirror; he bent me over the living room couch and fucked me from behind; he lay on the kitchen floor and watched me ride his cock until we both exploded.

One night as he was dozing off on the living room floor, exhausted from our marathon session, I whispered a suggestion in his ear.

"David, are you awake? Are you listening?"

"Mmmm . . . yes, I'm listening." He could barely keep his eyes open.

I played with the fine hairs on his chest. "I'd like to have sex someplace new and different. I think it would be very exciting for both of us. What about your office?"

That got his attention. His eyelids flew open. "That's a great idea. . . . I love it."

"Okay. The next time you're in your office, I want you to think about what you'd like to do with me there."

He rolled on top of me. I could feel his cock hardening. "I already have some ideas . . . and the thought of you in my office—naked and wet and ready for me—makes me incredibly hot."

I gave him a complacent smile and reached for his hard shaft. "Are we going to have a triple-header tonight? That's a first for us, I hope it's not the last time."

"Oh, honey, I want to make love to you all night long." This time he proceeded slowly, kissing my mouth and my throat, probing the sensitive folds of my ears with the tip of his tongue. I fondled my breasts until my nipples were hard. "Put your cock between my tits," I whispered. I squeezed my breasts together, and he slid his long shaft between them. I licked the head of his cock for a long time until I could taste drops of cum. He knelt between my legs, put his hands under my ass and thrust his shaft deep into my wet, warm pussy. He remained still, allowing me to hump his cock until we came at the same time. He collapsed onto my chest and sighed deeply. At that moment I knew that no woman had ever excited or satisfied him as much as I did.

11

David called me the following afternoon from his office. His voice was strained. "I haven't been able to concentrate, can't get anything done. I keep thinking about you, about having sex here. My cock has been rock hard all day long."

"Sorry for the inconvenience! I hope you haven't lost a lot of money," I teased.

"I will if I don't get some relief soon. Can you come over here this evening? Around eight o'clock, when everyone else has gone."

My nipples grew hard at the thought. "Yes . . . I'll come over and give you everything you want." He gave me the address and suite number. "See you soon," I whispered. "Only four hours from now. Keep thinking about me."

After we hung up I showered and shampooed and rubbed jasmine-scented lotion all over my body. I resisted the temptation to masturbate. I wanted to save my lust for the real encounter.

When I arrived at David's office building, I wasn't surprised by the understated elegance of the enormous lobby, but I still felt a twinge of intimidation. Even now, I wasn't completely accustomed to the extent of David's wealth and power.

I gave the security guard my name, and he waved me through immediately. I took the elevator up to the forty-second floor, my body tingling with excitement.

When the elevator doors slid open, David was standing there, waiting for me impatiently. "Kiss?" I asked. He wrapped his strong arms around me and kissed me hard, his tongue probing the depths of my mouth. I collapsed against his chest.

He let go abruptly. "Come this way," he said, pulling me by the hand down the silent, darkened hallways to his office.

An enormous teak desk with an Italian leather office chair. Decadently plush blue carpeting, so deep and soft my spike heels sank in more than an inch. Spectacular views of midtown twinkling through the windows. Oh, this place had endless erotic possibilities.

David undressed me very slowly, skimming his hands over my throat, my shoulders, my breasts. My blouse, my bra, my skirt fell to the floor until I was standing only in my panties, stockings and high heels.

"Don't move," he ordered. "I want to look at you." He stared at me as he undid the knot of his gray silk tie and slid it from his collar. "Turn around."

I obeyed, feeling a deep thrill rush through my body. He tied my hands behind my back and then stood behind me, grinding his hard-on against my ass while he fondled my breasts.

"Do you like that, Gillian?" he whispered

"God, yes." I sighed. "Please play with my pussy. Make me wet."

His hand crept down to my crotch. He used a single finger to massage my clit through the black lace.

"Yes . . . that feels so good. Please don't stop, David. Please make me come. . . ."

He removed his hand. "Not yet, darling. I'm going to make you wait."

I knew this was payback for the first time in my new apartment, when I had forced him to wait and watch me play with myself. He guided me over to his office chair and sat down with me facing him. My wet pussy was just inches from his face.

He kissed my lips and clit through the lacy fabric—again and again. I moaned and undulated against his mouth. I longed to hold his head against my pussy, but I was helpless with my hands tied behind my back.

He slowly pulled my panties down to my knees. He flicked his tongue just once against my swollen clit.

"David, please . . . I'm begging you . . . let me come."

"All in good time, darling." He continued to tease me gently with his tongue and then slid two fingers into my warm pussy. He increased the pressure of his tongue while he pumped his fingers in and out of my pussy.

"Lick harder . . . please lick harder. . . ." I came intensely, closing my eyes and crying out in the ecstasy of the moment.

"Very nice," David murmured. He unzipped his fly and released his long, hard shaft. "Do you want to suck it, darling?"

"Yes," I panted.

"Say it. Tell me exactly what you want to do."

"I want to suck your cock. I want to lick the head and the shaft and your balls until you can't stand it anymore." I dropped to my knees and licked furiously, my tongue bathing every inch of his cock. Then I opened my mouth. David slid the shaft all the way in and then gently pulled my head back and forth as I sucked. He moaned with pleasure.

After a few minutes he lifted me up. He braced the chair against the desk and bent me over, spreading my legs wide. He stood behind me and caressed my ass. I waited with a sharp sense of anticipation. When I least expected it, he thrust his cock hard into my pussy, making me gasp with pleasure and surprise.

He stood perfectly still. "Move your hips, Gillian. Hump my cock," he ordered.

I rocked in a slow rhythm. David remained motionless until we were both on the brink. Then he bucked wildly, groaning harshly as he spurted. My body shuddered with another overwhelming orgasm.

David's office became our new favorite erotic setting. A few times he called me in the middle of the day and asked me—almost desperately—to come over. I always raced over there. He'd lock the office door, but knowing that dozens of people were just yards away titillated both of us. I loved to lie on the smooth, cool surface of his desk and watch him work on me—tantalizing me with his tongue and fingers until I completely lost control. Sometimes he would sit in his office chair with me standing before him, hands on his shoulders. He would slide his silk tie back and forth between my legs; the friction against my clit and lips made me come intensely—a completely new and different kind of orgasm.

After we were finished I would dress and leave, wishing his prim assistant, Ms. Stone, a good afternoon as I passed through the reception area. She always gave me a tight-lipped smile. Of course she knew what David and I had just done—I must have reeked of sex, and the goofy, satisfied look on my face was a dead giveaway. I suspected that Ms. Stone's feelings for David were much warmer than the ordinary devotion an assistant had for her boss. I knew she probably considered me a slut, but I didn't care.

One afternoon I had lunch with Steve at a fabulous new sushi restaurant. I told him about my reconciliation with David and mentioned Ms. Stone's attachment to her boss.

"Do you think this woman is a threat?" Steve asked.

I shrugged. "Not unless David has a thing for motherly types. Ms. Stone must be in her early sixties."

"Sounds like you have nothing to worry about. David probably doesn't even notice other women when you're around."

I slapped him lightly on the arm. "Save the Southern charm for Oliver!"

Work continued to go well. The second radio-station commercial was a big hit; posters of me plugging WROL started popping up—on billboards, on the sides of busses, in subway stations. It was weird to see my wide-eyed, grinning face everywhere. "I look like a demented chipmunk," I groaned to Anita.

"You look adorable," she countered.

I landed a few more parts in commercials and minor roles in TV shows. Steve told me the writers for *Nights of Passion* were creating some new female roles; he promised to put in a good word for me with the casting director and producers.

I was able to afford more new furniture for my apartment. I replaced the old orange couch with a comfy sofa and love seat covered in soft, pale green fabric. I also bought a brass bed frame; David loved to tie my wrists to the headboard and watch me moan and writhe under his skilled hands.

One night he surprised me by asking me to tie him up. I thought that he always wanted to be the dominant one—but I was excited by the idea of role reversal. I undressed him slowly and used a silk scarf to secure his hands behind his back. He stood in front of my full-length mirror with his hard cock standing at attention. I stripped down to my panties, pressed my hard nipples against his chest and caressed his ass.

"Your cock is so hard," I murmured. "Do you want me to suck it?"

"Yes, Gillian. I want that very much."

"You have to please me first."

I pushed him down on his knees. He stared as I rubbed my lips and clit through my panties. I slid two fingers under the elastic and into my wet opening. I held my fingers to his mouth. "Lick my juice off my fingers."

He obeyed, relishing the taste. I slowly pulled my panties down and spread my lips.

"Would you like to eat my pussy?"

"Oh, yes," he moaned. "Your pussy is so sweet."

"Kiss it first."

He pressed his warm, full lips against my clit, kissing me over and over. I whimpered in delight and rubbed my pussy all over his face; my juice made his skin glisten. Then I told him to lick, his tongue lapped furiously until I was on the brink. He took my clit between his lips and sucked gently.

I pulled away before he could make me come. I made him stand again and then dropped to my knees. "I think you've earned a good tongue lashing," I said. I used my tongue, lips and teeth delicately on his shaft and balls. He panted as he watched our reflection in the mirror. I saw him grit his teeth, trying to hold back his orgasm. I kneeled between his legs and slid my tongue from his balls all the way up the crack of his ass—back and forth, back and forth. He closed his eyes and moaned my name.

I pushed him down into a chair and straddled his lap. I spread my lips and rubbed the head of his cock against my engorged clit. "Do you want me to slide your cock inside?" I whispered.

"Yes, please. . . ."

"Beg harder."

"*Please*, Gillian, I want your pussy so much. . . . Please put my cock in."

I slowly lowered my pussy onto his cock. I sat still for several minutes until he begged me to fuck him.

I rocked gently at first and then increased the tempo. I

gripped his shoulders and humped his cock as fast and as hard as I could. A deep orgasm possessed my body; I could hear my cries mingling with David's as he exploded inside me.

I rested my head against his chest as we both recovered slowly. I pushed my sweaty hair away from my face and smiled at David. "I kind of like having you as a personal sex slave. You're so well qualified for the position."

He laughed and gently bit my left nipple. "I'll be your slave anytime."

I thought my life couldn't get any better. Then one night, out of the blue, David dropped the bombshell.

We were lying in my bed, drinking red wine and lazing away the time as we waited for David to get hard again.

He gave me a sideways glance. "Gillian, I'd love to share a fantasy with you."

I smiled and leaned closer to nuzzle his neck. "Great. You know I love to hear about your fantasies."

"Well, this one is a little . . . unusual." He actually seemed a bit nervous—David, who was always supremely self-confident.

"Go ahead and tell me," I coaxed. "You know I'm pretty open-minded."

"Okay." For a moment he seemed as shy and as self-conscious as I often was. "Please don't be offended. . . . I'd like to watch you having sex with another man," he blurted out.

I tried to conceal my shock. "Watch me have sex with another man?" I wasn't sure I'd heard him correctly.

"Yes. It's a fantasy I've had for a long time."

"I see." I didn't know how to react. An image of Steve and Oliver flashed through my mind. "Do you want to . . . join in?"

"No. I just want to watch the two of you." My nipples stiffened as he brushed his fingertips across my breasts. "It would be a huge turn-on for me, Gillian."

"I don't know . . ."

"Look, we can do it just once. I think you'd really like it." His tone was persuasive.

"I'm extremely picky about sex partners," I pointed out. "I don't just jump into bed with a man—well, you were the exception. This guy would have to be good-looking and great in bed and discreet—"

"Greg is very good-looking, and I'm sure he's a talented lover. I've known him for a while, and he's definitely discreet."

"You actually have someone in mind?" This was getting weirder and weirder.

"Yes. Greg is a personal trainer at my gym. He's an actor like you, actually, just moonlighting at the gym to make some money. Of course, he's in great shape. And he's definitely interested."

I felt a flash of anger. "You told this guy about me? Did you describe what I'm like in bed?"

"No, honey, no," David said soothingly. "I had a beer with him one night after a training session. I mentioned that I had this fantasy and I knew a woman who might also be into it. He was turned on by the idea."

"Oh. I see," I said dubiously. "I'm still not sure, David. You know I love to please you in bed, but I've never done anything like that."

"Think about it, okay? Just once. . . . It would be very exciting, Gillian." He ran his tongue from my throat down to the peaks of my nipples. I felt the familiar rush of warmth between my legs. At that moment I thought I'd do anything this man wanted.

I debated the idea for days. I didn't tell Anita, Steve or anyone else about David's fantasy. I kept Miss Prudence and Miss Hornypants out of the debate, but I still seesawed between saying yes and saying no. One moment I'd think, *Why not? The idea does make me kind of hot. I'm young and single—now is the time for sexual adventure. I'm not going to do this kind of thing when I'm thirty-five and have three kids.* Then a moment later I'd feel completely repulsed by the notion. *It's just too strange. And if I tell David yes, what will he come up with next? He might want to watch me having sex with another woman—or engage in some other kinky fantasy. It might just destroy our affair.*

David didn't pressure me, but I knew he was thinking about this fantasy every time we had sex. I wondered if he might lose patience eventually—dump me and find another lover who would indulge him. There were so many beautiful women in the city who would gladly cater to his every whim.

One morning I woke up feeling especially horny. I closed my eyes and masturbated, thinking about David's fantasy . . . a handsome young man sucking my nipples, rubbing my clit, fucking me . . . David watching us with those intense blue eyes and stroking his cock . . . the three of us coming simultaneously . . . God, it was hot. I came hard, screaming into my pillow.

After I had recovered, I called David's cell. Damnit—voice mail again. "Okay, I'll do it," I said simply and hung up.

He called me back almost immediately. "Do you mean it, Gillian?"

"Yes. But you have to agree to certain conditions."

"Of course. Anything you want."

"Okay. I want you to bring him over here. We'll spend a little time together. If I decide I don't want to go through with it, I'll give you a signal—scratch my forehead or something. That will mean it's off, and both of you should leave. And you're not allowed to get angry if I decide I don't want to do it."

"I won't be angry, Gillian, I promise. Thanks for saying you'll give it a try."

I felt a strong flutter of anxiety in my throat. Had I just

made the biggest mistake of my life? "Call Greg now and set it up. I might change my mind if we wait too long."

"Okay, I'll call you back as soon as I've talked to him."

We hung up. I sat on my bed in a daze, chewing my nails and wondering how it would all turn out.

12

David called me the next day to say he'd arranged for Greg to meet us at my apartment the following Saturday night. "Okay, sounds good," I squeaked.

My anxiety increased over the next few days. *What if this Greg guy is some kind of Neanderthal? What if I back out at the very last minute and David breaks his promise about not getting angry? What if the whole thing is a huge turn-off for all three of us?* I chewed my nails down to little stubs. *Very sexy*, I thought ruefully. I treated myself to an expensive manicure to prevent further gnawing.

I was dying to talk to Anita or Steve about the situation but couldn't bring myself to do it. Both of them had their wild ways, but I was sure they would be shocked at the idea of sweet little Gillian participating in a ménage à trois. I couldn't reach Anita, anyway. She'd gone to Costa Rica for a fashion shoot and wouldn't be back for several days.

On Saturday morning I tried to distract myself by cleaning the apartment, doing laundry, paying bills—any mundane chore to keep my mind off the coming night. In the afternoon I washed my hair, shaved, slathered on body lotion. I stared into my closet, wondering what on earth to wear for a minor orgy. Not the sweet Violette nightie David had given to me. Not the sexy black negligee I'd bought for myself. Jeans? The red tartan plaid dress? Nothing seemed right.

I finally settled on a black V-neck sweater and my short black skirt. A little sexy but nothing outrageous. I tried to read a novel and ignore the ticking clock as I waited for David's arrival. We had agreed that he'd come over and spend some time with me before Greg arrived.

I nearly hit the ceiling when I heard David's knock on the door. I opened it to find him looking handsomer and more charming than ever. He was holding a shopping bag. "Champagne," he said as he stepped into the living room. "I thought it might help us relax."

"Great idea," I said. "I don't have champagne flutes, but I think we can survive with wineglasses."

He followed me into the kitchen. My hands trembled slightly as I took three glasses from the cabinet. David pulled bottles of chilled Cristal from the bag. He expertly uncorked one bottle and filled two glasses.

I tossed back my champagne in a single gulp. "Hey, slow down." David laughed. "You don't want to get snockered so early in the evening."

"Sorry," I mumbled. "I am pretty nervous."

David poured me a second glass. "Let's take this bottle and the glasses into the living room. I'll help you calm down."

I sat on the couch and slowly sipped my champagne. I was pretty dizzy—I'd been too anxious to eat all day. The champagne hit me hard. *God, I hope I don't throw up—that would certainly spoil the mood.*

David stroked my hair and massaged my neck. "It's going to be fine, Gillian . . . it's going to be great."

I felt like a scared puppy being soothed by her master. "Okay.

Sure. Fine," I said, trying to enunciate clearly. "We have to decide on a signal. If I scratch my forehead, that means I don't want to do it and it's all off."

David smiled and brushed a strand of hair from my eyes. "Yes, ma'am. And if you lick your lips lasciviously, what will that signal?"

I giggled. The champagne was really getting to me. "That means full speed ahead!"

The loud buzz of the intercom made me jump. "Stay put," David ordered. "I'll get it."

I refilled my glass as he answered the intercom and buzzed—what was his name again?—Greg into the building.

I remained on the couch, swallowing hard as I watched David answer the door. A very tall, dark-haired young man entered the room.

I stood up, suddenly feeling stiff and formal. David turned to me. "Gillian, this is Greg. Greg, this is Gillian."

"Very nice to meet you," I said, feeling absurd.

"Nice to meet you, too, Gillian," he replied. We stood there awkwardly for a moment. *Do we shake hands or hug or what?* I wondered.

Greg seemed to feel as clueless as I did. We continued to just stand and look at each other. David hadn't exaggerated; Greg was very handsome. Probably in his late twenties.Very tall, even taller than David. Dark curly hair, olive skin, a high forehead, deep brown eyes. I guessed at a Mediterranean background. He was muscular but not in a gross, steroid-induced, bulging way.

"Greg, let me take your jacket and get you a glass of champagne," said David.

"Thanks." Greg shrugged off his jacket and handed it to him. David draped it on the back of a chair and went to the kitchen for more champagne.

"Have a seat," I said, trying hard to keep a quaver out of my voice. I sat on the couch, and he sat opposite me on the love seat. We smiled tentatively at each other until David returned with another bottle of Cristal and a third glass. David sat in a rocking chair. *So weird*, I thought. *We're about to have an orgy, and we're sitting as far apart as possible.*

David and Greg sipped while I gulped. I gave a little hiccup. "Sorry." I blushed brightly and put down the glass. No more champagne for me.

The two of them talked about inconsequential things while I tried to stop the spinning feeling in my head. Then Greg turned to me and said, "I've seen your commercials for WROL, Gillian. Good job." He had a nice voice, the kind of intonation my acting coach had once described as "mellifluous."

"Thanks," I replied. "David mentioned that you're an actor, too. Have you done anything recently?"

"Not around here. I've been in LA for the past couple of years. I had some small parts in movies and TV shows—nothing you'd remember. I just moved to New York a few months ago."

"Oh." We had exhausted that topic.

A few minutes of silence. I noticed that Greg's leg was jittering nervously. *This is never going to work*, I thought. Then David broke the lull.

"Greg, don't you think Gillian is pretty?" he asked.

"She's not pretty. She's beautiful," Greg replied, turning to stare at me.

"Oh . . . thanks." Another bright blush suffused my face.

"Greg . . . why don't you sit next to her," David suggested in a too-casual voice.

"Okay." Greg moved to the couch and sat down a foot away from me. I felt a little panicky at his proximity. *I can't do this*, I thought. *Scratch your forehead—now!* But I didn't move.

"I'm sure Gillian would like a kiss," said David.

Greg turned to me with a questioning look. I felt as rigid as a corpse, but I gave him a small nod. I closed my eyes as he leaned forward and brushed his full lips against mine.

"That was nice . . . but why don't you give her a real kiss." I felt like Greg and I were performing a scene—two actors with David as the director.

I looked into Greg's dark, deep-set eyes to let him know I was willing. He moved closer and put his arms around me. *So strong*, I thought. He kissed me with increasing intensity until my mouth opened for his tongue. He felt so different from David—and he smelled so different—like fresh tomatoes ripening in the sun.

I became absorbed in the moment, lost in the kiss, consumed by Greg's exotic odor. I actually forgot about David's presence until I heard him whisper, "Yes, that's good. Very good."

I broke away from Greg's embrace and looked at David. He had unzipped his fly and was running his thumb over the head of his shaft. I glanced away quickly and allowed Greg to wrap his arms around me again.

We kissed for several more minutes. He tentatively brushed his fingertips against my breasts; my nipples immediately responded. The champagne made me feel languorous and sensual.

"Take off her sweater, Greg," said a far-off voice. Greg gently pulled the sweater over my head and then caressed my breasts through the thin silk of my bra. I felt a slow pulse beat harder between my thighs. I was as excited as I had ever been with David—but it wasn't the same at all.

Greg slowly pulled down the cups of my bra to expose my stiff pink nipples. I gave a little gasp as I felt his tongue flick softly over each peak. I closed my eyes again, abandoning myself to pleasure. Greg moved from one nipple to the other, sucking and gently biting as his large hands caressed my breasts. His touch was so subtle—so different from David's urgency.

I opened my eyes when Greg pulled his mouth away. He

stood and started unbuckling his belt. "No . . . let me," I whispered. I fumbled until the belt was undone and his fly was unzipped. I pulled his jeans to his knees and rubbed his enormous hard-on through his briefs. He closed his eyes and moaned.

I pulled down his briefs and wrapped my hand around his long, thick shaft. I licked the head until droplets of cum appeared. I lapped up the cum, savoring the taste, and then ran my tongue up and down his shaft. Finally I took his cock between my lips, pressing my palms against his ass. He slid the shaft all the way in and then slowly pumped his cock in and out of my mouth. I moved my hands to his balls, gently squeezing and rubbing.

"That's it, Gillian . . . suck his cock." I glanced around to look at David. He was stroking his shaft fast, his eyes half closed in ecstasy. I suddenly thought, *I wish he weren't here*. I was startled by the realization. I closed my eyes and turned my attention back to Greg's cock.

Greg finally pulled his cock from my mouth and kneeled before me. He slowly pushed up my skirt. I spread my legs for him. He teased me through my panties with his tongue and his fingers until I couldn't stand it anymore. I yanked my panties down and tossed them aside. I spread my lips to show him how ready I was—my swollen clit and wet opening.

He wasn't as impatient as I was. He ran his silky tongue up the inside of my right thigh and then my left thigh. Goose bumps rose on my skin. I was breathing hard, my heart pounding. He finally flicked his tongue against my clit. A soft animal cry emerged from my throat. His tongue flickered a few more times across my clit and then he buried his tongue between my lips. I held his head, undulating against his mouth.

"Lick her pussy until she screams . . . she loves that."

David again. I blocked him out and completely lost myself in the sensation of Greg's tongue. I came explosively, digging my nails into his scalp. I fell back against the soft cushions, completely spent.

Greg cautiously slid his shaft into my pussy. He remained still for a few minutes, playing with my nipples until they hardened again. He stared into my eyes, and I watched a small smile curve his lips. I held his gaze and returned his smile.

He began to pump slowly. I felt a quivering sensation in my pussy. "You're going to make me come again," I whispered—so softly that David could not hear me.

"Yes, I want you to come again. I want to feel your pussy convulse around my cock. . . ." He thrust a little harder and deeper. I expelled a long sigh of bliss.

I rocked my hips and felt the pleasure increase, building to a crescendo. I gripped Greg's muscular forearms and felt a long, slow orgasm burst through me. At the same moment he gave one last deep thrust and groaned heavily. I felt his hot cum filling my pussy. A moment later I heard another deep groan. We both looked at David as he spurted, his face crumpled with passion.

Greg slowly slid his cock out of my pussy and stood. I closed my legs and sat up straight. David was busy with a handkerchief. The silence was the most awkward I'd ever heard.

Greg quickly yanked up his briefs and jeans. He zipped up and buckled his belt like a cartoon character in fast motion. "Look, I have to go," he said tensely. He avoided looking at me or David.

"Hey, the night is young. Stay a while," said David, giving Greg his most persuasive smile.

"No, really, I have to go." Greg grabbed his jacket off the chair and shrugged it on. "Sorry to be rude. Thanks for . . . everything." He quickly walked to the front door and was gone before I could even decide what to say.

I looked at David. A hot flash of anger passed over his face.

"Well, that was a little weird," I said.

He gave an annoyed shrug. "I don't know what his problem was."

I stood up, still feeling a little shaky from too much champagne and two intense orgasms. "At least you got your fantasy," I said. "I'm going to take a shower. Why don't you wait for me in the bedroom? We can have a second round—just the two of us." I wanted to break him out of his bad mood—and I wanted to get Greg out of my mind.

Despite my best intentions, I found myself thinking about Greg in the shower. I was still surprised that I had been so turned on by him. Sex with David was always so intense and exciting; I didn't think another man could ever give me so much pleasure.

I wrapped myself in a towel and found David waiting for me in bed, propped up against the headboard. He still looked sullen. I dropped the towel to the floor and struck an over-the-top pose, thrusting out my tits and ass and batting my eyelashes. He gave me a brief, reluctant smile.

I climbed into the bed and massaged his shoulders. "So it didn't go exactly the way you planned . . . still, it was good. I enjoyed it . . . and you obviously did, too."

David gave me a piercing glance. "Yes, you did enjoy it. A lot. Did Greg fuck you better than I do?"

I dropped my hands from his shoulders. "For god's sake, David. This was *your* fantasy. You wanted to watch me having sex with another man. I can't believe you're jealous," I snapped.

"Okay, okay, I'm sorry," said David. He didn't sound sincere, but I knew it was impossible to argue with him when he was in this kind of mood.

I snuggled against his chest, pressing my hard nipples against his. "Let's just forget about Greg, all right? I'm still very horny, and I need you to satisfy me. . . ."

David immediately went for my pussy, sliding his fingers in

and out. I was wet but not quite ready when he plunged his cock into me. He fucked me harder than he ever had before, clutching my ass, panting as rivulets of sweat dripped from his face. He was trying to prove something—his superiority. I closed my eyes and thought of Greg—his delicate touch, the warmth of his wet tongue. I finally came. David continued pounding me hard; he seemed ready to go on forever.

"You horny little bitch," he growled. "You need two big hard cocks . . . you need to get fucked all night long."

I was a little shocked, but I played along. "Yes, I'm so horny," I breathed into his ear. "I love to get fucked. I love to have two cocks. . . ."

He finally came, sounding like a man in exquisite pain.

A few minutes later he dressed and gave me a perfunctory kiss. "I need to get up early, so I should sleep at my place. I'll call you tomorrow," he said with that irritating trick of avoiding my eyes. For the first time I was glad to see him go.

I was still half drunk from the champagne. I fell asleep quickly, but my sleep was disturbed by a vivid, unsettling dream. I was sitting in a rowboat. Two men, one on each oar, were paddling, but the boat seemed to be spinning in circles. I didn't know where we were supposed to go, but I was worried we would never reach our destination. Then I heard a familiar voice calling from the shore. "Gillian!" Anita was waving her arms at me. "You have to pick one. One man." Confused, I looked at the men but couldn't make out their faces. Both seemed to be strangers. "How can I make a decision? It's impossible to choose," I called to Anita. But she was gone.

13

I woke up the next morning with a pounding headache and a furry tongue. *Too much fucking champagne*, I thought. I hadn't had a hangover in years; I'd forgotten how nasty it felt.

I closed my eyes again for a moment, hoping the throbbing in my head would subside. Memories of the previous night came floating back to me. Champagne . . . David . . . Greg . . . did it really happen, or was I remembering one of my disturbing dreams?

I staggered out to the living room. Empty Cristal bottles and glasses. *Yes, it did happen. Oh, god.*

I washed my face with icy cold water and made a pot of super-strong coffee. As the caffeine surged through my brain, I remembered details. Feeling so turned on by Greg, coming so intensely. Feeling annoyed by David's presence. Greg's abrupt departure and David's irritation. Sex with David, which I barely enjoyed. *You horny little bitch.* Sober and in the light of day, I felt really offended. David would hear about this.

My cell phone rang; the muted tone sounded like a jackhammer to me. For once, my phone telepathy failed me. Perhaps it was Greg? No, he didn't have my phone number. He probably didn't even remember my name. I flipped open the phone.

"It's Sandra." A cool voice, sophisticated and low-pitched.

My brain was still fuzzy. Sandra? A neighbor? Old high school friend? Someone from the temp agency? A casting director? I couldn't place her.

She didn't wait for me to respond. "Look, we got engaged over Christmas, and we're getting married in the spring. I told him he'd have to give you up. So it's over."

I was baffled. "You must have the wrong number. This is Gillian Monroe."

"I know who you are. I guess you don't know who I am. I'm Sandra Winthrop, David's fiancée."

"David? David Wentworth?" I said stupidly.

"Yes, David Wentworth," she answered impatiently. "And it's over. He's had enough of you. Don't try to contact him again."

I felt shock morph into rage. Who did this bitch think she was?

"Look, honey, I don't chase after David," I shouted. "He chases after me. He's obsessed with me. He calls me up and begs me to see him. Just my voice turns him on. He told me that sex with me is the best he's ever had. And you can be sure that when he's in bed with you, he's fantasizing about me." I slammed the phone shut and tossed it on the kitchen counter.

Then I burst into tears. David *engaged* . . . I just couldn't believe it. But it had to be true. Why would that woman lie to me? I'd been so blind, so stupid—and that bastard David had used me.

I desperately needed to talk to someone. I started to dial Anita's number when I remembered that she was in Costa Rica until next week. Aunt Mary? Mom? Caroline? I couldn't talk to any of them about this bizarre and humiliating turn of events.

I dialed Steve's number.

* * *

Twenty minutes later Steve was sitting at my kitchen table, stroking my hair while I ranted and cried. "I just can't believe how stupid I was," I raged. "Of course it all makes sense now. He hardly ever spent the night with me. I always got his voice mail when I called his cell. Those business trips to Boston—he didn't want me to come with him. *She* was probably with him. And of course he didn't get me a Christmas present—he was too busy shopping for an engagement ring. Even this apartment," I flung an arm wide in a gesture of disgust, "I thought it was a generous gift. But he just wanted to come here so Sandra wouldn't catch us at his penthouse."

I was overwhelmed by a fresh torrent of tears. "God, Gillian, I'm so sorry," said Steve. He pulled me to my feet and into his embrace. He held me tight until my sobs subsided into hiccups. He poured me a glass of water and handed it to me. I downed it in a few gulps.

I rubbed my swollen eyes. "Thanks, Steve, you're such a good friend. I'm not really brokenhearted, just totally shocked and humiliated. I should have known I was just David's piece of ass on the side . . . his little sex toy. Aunt Mary warned me that he had a reputation for being ruthless, but I ignored her."

I had never seen Steve look so angry before. "David Wentworth is a first-class asshole," he said. "And I bet a lot of people let him get away with it."

I sniffled. "Well, I'm certainly not going to let him behave like an asshole this time. I'm going to give that bastard hell. . . ." I picked up my cell phone, but Steve snatched it from my hand.

"Wait, Gillian. Of course you have to break it off, but perhaps you should wait a day or so. You're still pretty upset and vulnerable—better to wait until you've calmed down."

"I guess you're right." I rubbed my tear-stained face. "God, I feel like crap, and I must look like supercrap."

Steve laughed. "Well, I have seen you looking better. Why

don't you take a shower and get dressed? Come over to our place. Oliver and I just got *Gone With the Wind* on DVD, we planned to laze around today. Oliver is going to make his killer asparagus pepperjack quiche."

I flung my arms around his neck and rested my head against his chest. "That's so nice, Steve. I'd like that. I need some distraction—and some good company."

Scarlett's travails made my own seem laughably inconsequential. I thought I'd be too upset to eat anything, but I scarfed down two slices of Oliver's incredible quiche. A glass of chardonnay took the edge off my hangover.

I talked to Oliver in depth for the first time. He was so funny and sweet—I could see why Steve loved him. "I know you guys have probably heard this before." I sighed. "But I wish there were more straight men like you around."

I kissed them both good night. On the taxi ride home, I felt almost happy. So it was over with David. Big deal. I deserved better—and I would find it.

I had slipped on my nightie and crawled into bed, when my cell phone rang. I felt a surge of irritation. Who could be calling at 11:30? If it was that bitch Sandra again—

"Gillian, don't hang up."

David. *Shit.*

"What do you want?" I snarled.

"Look. I know Sandra called you. I'm sorry about that. But she won't change anything between us—"

"Are you out of your fucking mind?"

"Don't be mad. We can still see each other. We just have to be very discreet. Gillian, you know how much I want you—and I know how much you want me—"

"You lying, sneaking, selfish son of a bitch. You are never going to touch me again." I snapped the phone shut.

I turned the ringer off, but I lay awake for hours, wondering if David would try to call me again.

I slept fitfully. I was exhausted the next day. I tried to recapture the feeling of relief and bravado I'd experienced after my evening with Steve and Oliver, but I just felt drained. I gave myself little projects to keep my mind occupied—cleaning out my closets, repotting an unhappy-looking fern, polishing a silver necklace and bracelet. I thought about shopping for a new rug and shower curtain—my old red rug and curtain clashed with the yellow walls of the bathroom in my new apartment. I suddenly froze as I realized something. *What if David decides to kick me out of the apartment? I wouldn't put it past him. That would be the cherry on top of his betrayal.*

Anita returned from Costa Rica and stopped by my apartment, looking gorgeously tanned and fit. She was horrified when I told her about Sandra. "Oh, god, Gillian, I feel responsible."

"How are you responsible? You didn't make David act like a jerk."

"But I kept encouraging you to just enjoy this . . . thing with him. I should have known he was using you."

"You couldn't have known. I'm the one who should have seen through him. But he was always so charming . . . and he seemed to want me so much. I can't believe that the whole time, he was sleeping with another woman. And proposing to another woman. . . ."

My voice trailed off as tears stung my eyes. "God, Anita. It still hurts. I was good enough to fuck but not good enough for anything else."

Anita held me tight as the tears broke loose again. Damnit, when would the pain and shock go away?

* * *

Anita, Steve and Oliver were godsends. Over the next few weeks, they worked hard to distract me. I spent a day on the set on *Nights of Passion* with Steve and Oliver. We had a blast. "Yes, please, I'd love to be on this show!" I told them. "We'll get you on, I promise," said Steve. "Even if it's for only a single episode."

Anita came over frequently and took me shopping. We spent a weekend in Hanover skiing and hanging out with old high school friends. In a fit of generosity, I invited Caroline to visit me in New York for a weekend. She jumped at the invitation. "She'll probably drive me crazy," I moaned to Anita later. "I love my sister, but we drive each other up the wall if we spend too much time together."

"I'll run interference," promised Anita. "If the three of us go out together, perhaps you two won't grate on each other so much."

"You're a saint," I said. Anita snorted in derision.

I kept expecting David to call me again—or write or send flowers—and I steeled myself against his persuasive charm. I mentally rehearsed several versions of a kiss-off—which all featured every obscenity I had ever heard. But there was no word from him.

I struggled against the temptation to call him; several times I started to dial his number and had to sternly lecture myself to stop. Forgetting David was a much greater challenge than I had thought it would be. I kept remembering the fun we had and the tender moments—and the sex. I was horny all the time. I masturbated constantly, and it was so hard to keep David out of my fantasies. I tried to replace him with Viggo Mortensen, Heath Ledger, Johnny Depp, my high school crush . . . none of them worked. Only one man was able to distract me from memories of David. Greg. I remembered that sweetly passionate encounter in every detail—his dark, soulful eyes and electrifying touch; the warmth of his flickering tongue against my nipples and clit . . .

I longed to see him again—but that was impossible. *I don't know how to reach him—and why would he want to see me again, anyway? He probably thinks of me as a slut—David's slut.*

I reached a low point when I saw a short piece about David's engagement in a daily tabloid. He was pictured with his fiancée, Sandra Winthrop. She was from an old Boston Brahman family—ancestors came over on the Mayflower and all that crap. A lot of old family money, too, I was sure—how convenient for David. She was an interior designer who had worked on the lobby decor for David's new luxury condo building. (So he *had* been with her in Boston. All those times we had shared incredible phone sex—I bit my lip.) I studied the photo. She was very beautiful—in a vulpine kind of way. Extremely tall and superthin. Sleek auburn bob. Hard dark eyes. About as different from me as any woman could be. I couldn't stand to look at David's face in the photo.

I did get a kind of smug satisfaction from the knowledge that it was probably worse for him. The ads for WROL were everywhere, my face was all over the city. I hoped David was plagued by memories that made him hard—and full of regrets.

Aunt Mary called. She'd heard about David's engagement. She came to Manhattan and invited me out for coffee, giving me a look of deep sympathy as we sat on the sofa at Java Java.

"I should have listened to you. You were right to warn me off him." I sighed.

"I don't think anyone could have persuaded you to say no to that man." Mary gave me a rueful smile. "You know, years ago when I was in my early twenties—I think it was back in the Jurassic age—I had an affair with a man like David. Rich, powerful, magnetic. Even worse, Evan was married—and I knew it. I wanted him anyway. We had a stormy relationship that dragged on for months. I kept breaking it off; he kept chasing me. Like an idiot I'd let him suck me back into the affair. I thought I'd never get away from him."

"How did it finally end?"

"I moved to Los Angeles for a year. I absolutely hated it out there, but I knew it was the only way to get free of that bastard. It worked. When I returned to New York, he was having an affair with my best friend Lila. Well, my former best friend. I had to stay away from her, too. In the end I missed Lila more than I missed Evan."

I gazed pensively into my coffee mug. "God, I hope I don't have to take such drastic measures. Well, I haven't heard from David in weeks, so he probably doesn't want me anymore."

Mary raised her eyebrows. "I doubt that. But if he tries to contact you again, stay strong. The only way to quit a man like David is cold turkey. It's like kicking heroin."

I decided that this time I would follow Mary's advice.

I gained eight pounds without even thinking about it. I finally resolved to yank myself out of the sloth of depression. I embarked on an intense fitness program, jogging with Anita nearly every morning; going to the gym nearly every afternoon; cutting sugar, salt and alcohol from my diet completely. The grueling regime focused my attention away from David and my raging lust.

I continued to land small parts in commercials and TV shows; I also won a supporting role in a new off–Broadway comedy, *Final Thoughts*. It was scheduled to run for only three weeks, but I loved the script and was grateful for the distraction of work.

I never heard from Wentworth Properties about my lease. I wondered: *Perhaps David decided to throw me a small bone of consolation—or maybe he really has forgotten about me.*

* * *

Anita and I spent Valentine's Day at my apartment. We watched both Bridget Jones movies on DVD and polished off a pint of Häagen-Dazs mint chocolate chip. It was the first sugar I'd tasted in weeks—the only indulgence I'd allowed myself in a very long time.

My mood was a little self-indulgent as well. "Well, this is a bit of a downer," I said. "Last Valentine's Day we were alone, too. I hadn't met Steve or David yet. And you were on hiatus from Michael."

"True," replied Anita, licking the last bit of ice cream off her spoon. "But I'd rather be alone than with jerks like David or Michael—or with a closeted gay guy like Steve."

"I suppose you're right." I heaved a dramatic sigh. "But what's wrong with us, Anita? I mean, even a screw-up like Bridget Jones can find true love. Why can't we?"

"Bridget is a fictional character. This is real life," Anita said. "Amazing guys aren't going to just drop down from the sky. We've had time to recover from our wounds. We need to get back into the jungle of love."

Anita and I started going out again—to clubs, parties, trendy new restaurants—any place where hot, single guys might be. I was skittish and turned down several guys who asked me for a date. But it felt good to know that I could still catch the eye of an attractive man. My heart and my ego were slowly healing, and I knew that soon I'd be ready to take the plunge.

My life seemed to be on the upswing again. And then—once again—fate slapped me upside the head. One afternoon I came home from a jog; I was stripping off my sweaty workout clothes when my cell phone rang. I answered it and heard a vaguely familiar voice say my name.

"Gillian? This is Elizabeth Stone. David Wentworth's assistant."

I stiffened immediately. "I don't want to talk to David. Or see him."

"He doesn't know I've called you. Look, I just need to talk with you. . . . Could you spare fifteen minutes this afternoon? We can meet for coffee—anyplace that's convenient for you."

I felt a little dizzy. It took me a moment to pull myself together. "Look, Ms. Stone, I really don't know what we could possibly have to talk about—"

"Please, Gillian," she said. There was a begging note in her voice. "It's really important."

I was startled by her urgency—and more than a little curious. "Okay. I can give you fifteen minutes." I gave her the address for Java Java.

When I entered Java Java, Elizabeth Stone was waiting for me, sitting ramrod straight at a table. Her appearance was immaculate, as always—perfectly coiffed silver-blond hair, discreet makeup, a navy-blue suit and snow-white blouse without a single wrinkle. She reminded me of a photo of a "career girl" from a 1950s fashion magazine.

"Thank you for agreeing to meet me," she said as I plopped down on the opposite chair.

"You're welcome, Ms. Stone."

"Please, call me Elizabeth." She gave me her tight, thin-lipped smile.

"Okay, Elizabeth. Now why did you want to talk to me?"

She carefully poured half a tablespoon of cream into her coffee. "It's about David—of course."

We were interrupted by a waitress who took my order for a latte. After she'd gone, I turned my attention back to Elizabeth. "Well, I figured as much. But as I'm sure you know, I've had no contact with David for weeks. And I intend to keep it that way."

"Yes, I know. And I know that David didn't treat you very well."

I snorted. "That's an understatement. He lied to me, deceived me, used me—"

"I know, I know. But David had feelings for you. He still does."

We were briefly interrupted by the reappearance of the waitress. I waited until she'd placed my latte on the table and sashayed away.

"I really don't care about David's feelings at this point." I sounded harsh, almost bitchy. *Good.*

Elizabeth leaned forward and locked her eyes with mine. "This engagement to Sandra Winthrop is the worst thing that could have happened to David. I know her. She's a manipulative witch—perhaps even a sociopath. She practically forced him into proposing to her, and she'll make him miserable. You're the only one who might be able to break up the engagement."

I was silent for a moment. Finally I said, "Elizabeth, tell me something . . . how long have you worked for David?"

"Nearly thirteen years. I was there at the beginning, when he was working out of a tiny one-room office on West Forty-Third Street."

"And how long have you been in love with David?"

Her cool reserve was shaken—but only for a moment. She gave me another tight smile. "Nearly thirteen years. Of course I know that any romantic relationship with David is impossible . . . but I can't kill my feelings for him."

"I'm sorry, Elizabeth. I'm sorry you're in love with that cold bastard. And I'm sorry I can't help you save him from Sandra's clutches. But my feelings for him are dead."

I threw a five-dollar bill on the table, picked up my purse and left without a backward glance.

* * *

"My god, the melodrama never ends," said Anita when I called to tell her about my meeting with Elizabeth Stone. "I've watched soap operas with fewer surprises."

"I know. I keep thinking David is gone from my life forever, but he keeps popping back in." I sighed. "I think I've solved one mystery. I wondered how Sandra found out about me and obtained my cell number. I bet Elizabeth tipped her off—probably anonymously."

"This Stone woman sounds conniving."

"I don't know if I'd describe her that way. She's clever but a bit pathetic. I really meant it when I told Elizabeth that I felt sorry for her. Imagine experiencing that kind of unrequited love for years. And you know, I actually feel a little sorry for Sandra. She made David promise to give me up, but obviously he never intended to do so. He'll keep lying to her and cheating on her. He'll never even try to be faithful. And now I wonder about Anna . . . I think I told you about her."

"David's ex-wife? The alcoholic?"

"Yep. I don't know if he actually drove her to drink, but I doubt he was very supportive once she developed the problem. That man is really good at spreading unhappiness."

"I think Sandra actually did you a favor," Anita pointed out. "Who knows how long you might have been entangled with this son of a bitch if she hadn't shown up."

"You're right. My affair with David could have dragged on for years. Thank god it ended when it did."

After I hung up, I remained on the couch for a few moments with my eyes closed, trying to identify a new feeling, one I'd never felt before in connection with David. It finally came to me: *relief*.

14

A few nights later, Anita and I were invited to a party by my new neighbor Natalie. Natalie was a petite redheaded whirlwind who worked in advertising but dreamed of starting an exclusive dating service. She bragged to me that she'd set up four couples who were still dating. "One couple is on the verge of engagement," she claimed. She added, "It should be easy to find great matches for beauties like you and Anita."

Anita and I were both dubious, but I pointed out that if the party stank we could just slip out of Natalie's apartment and down the hall to my place. We arrived at Natalie's with a bottle of white wine and could barely squeeze into the foyer. The place was infested with young, attractive and hopefully single men and women.

"Not bad," Anita whispered to me. "I already see some definite possibilities."

Anita looked marvelous in a short, slinky red dress and gold stilettos that made her tower over everyone else. As usual, nearly every man flocked to her side. Natalie and the other women looked extremely annoyed. I just smiled and shrugged—I was used to standing in Anita's shadow. One of the few men who didn't join in the worship of Anita smiled at me from across the room. I smiled back. He was very cute—rather short but with sharply defined features and silky blond hair. The handsome stranger carefully made his way through the crowd until he was standing next to me. "Hi, I'm Justin Willard." He had to lean down and speak directly into my ear to be heard.

"Gillian Monroe," I replied. "How are you?"

"Great, thanks. It's kind of hard to have a conversation in here, though—too many people, and Natalie has the music cranked up too loud. Do you want to go out on the fire escape?"

"Sure." I followed him through the crowd, tingling with that lovely anticipation you feel only at the beginning of a possible new romance.

Justin clambered through the kitchen window and held a hand out to help me onto the fire escape. We sat down, and I shivered a little. It was late March; still pretty cold.

"Here, take this." Justin shrugged off his jacket and handed it to me.

"Thanks, that's very gallant. But I don't want you freeze—"

"I'll be fine, really. I'm originally from Minnesota. This weather feels positively balmy to me."

I gave him my best smile as I put on the jacket and hugged my arms around my waist.

"So, Justin from Minnesota . . . what do you do?"

We exchanged our background data. He had graduated from law school just a year earlier and had been hired by a big New York firm. "Of course I'm basically an indentured servant at this point—I work obscenely long hours—but I love the law, and I'm pretty happy at the firm."

I talked about my acting career. "I knew you looked familiar," he said. "You're that really hot girl from the commercials for WROL. Can I have your autograph?"

I laughed. "Sure. Maybe I should write it in lipstick on your chest—that will give your fellow legal eagles something to talk about."

We talked for nearly half an hour. I loved his sense of humor; he was effortlessly funny. I laughed more than I had in months.

I finally suggested going back inside when I noticed Justin's lips turning blue. We returned to the living room to find it somewhat less crowded. Anita was still surrounded by her admirers, but she noticed me with Justin. "Very nice," she mouthed to me. I winked at her.

Justin and I continued our conversation for another hour. I downed three glasses of wine and felt my horniness increase with my blood alcohol level. *"Don't jump into bed with this one,"* Miss Prudence warned. *"Keep your head."* I tried to ignore the tingling sensation that crept from my belly to my pussy when Justin touched my hand.

The party started to wind down; guests left in pairs and then in small groups. I yawned. "Sorry, Justin. I guess I should go back to my place soon."

"Yeah, me, too. I'd like to go out with you sometime, Gillian. Could I have your number?"

I was thrilled. "Of course. I'd love to go out with you." I gave him my number and hoped he'd follow through.

He walked me and Anita down the hall to my apartment. At my door he gave me a good-night peck on the cheek. The tingling in my pussy became a full-strength throbbing.

"That guy is hunkalicious," said Anita as soon as I had locked the door behind us. "Maybe Justin is the one for you."

"I hope it's true." I sighed. "I have been feeling lonely lately . . . not to mention incredibly horny."

Anita laughed. "I know that feeling all too well. I gave my number to two guys—Rick and Lorenzo. I hope that at least one of them turns out to be decent."

Anita spent the night at my apartment. We shared my big

brass bed, whispering and giggling long into the night, just like we did in junior high.

I woke up the next morning feeling happier and more hopeful than I had in a long time. I made cheese and tomato omelets for breakfast; Anita and I wolfed them down. When my cell phone rang, I hoped it was Justin but decided that was unlikely. I gave Anita a thumbs-up when I heard his voice.

I agreed to meet him for dinner that night at a new Mexican restaurant a few blocks from my building. I felt the almost forgotten thrill of anticipation. Anita helped me pick out my outfit for the date—a jade-green wool skirt with a sexy slit up the side and black cashmere sweater with high, black leather boots. I felt a pang when I remembered that night so many months ago when she had helped me dress for my first date with David. I forced the memory out of my mind.

"Omelets and Mexican food . . . I'd better skip lunch and hit the gym this afternoon," I said to Anita. She persuaded me to jog with her instead. I met her at a west-side entrance to Central Park, and we ran nearly five miles. Trying to keep up with her long-legged gait nearly killed me, but the strenuous exercise made me feel virtuous.

I met Justin at the Mexican restaurant at seven. I felt pretty and confident. Justin looked great in a casual but elegant dark blue suit. I was so glad I had turned down the other guys I'd met over the last few months. Justin was worth the wait.

The food was so good I abandoned all pretense of daintiness. Justin and I each consumed two very strong margaritas and laughed a lot. I declined when Justin offered to order another round. I wanted to remain somewhat in control.

After dinner, Justin walked me back to my apartment. At my door he wrapped his arms around me as I leaned into his embrace. His smell was a little overwhelming—too much sickly sweet cologne or aftershave. I focused on the pressure of his lips against mine. He forced his tongue deep into my mouth—I was taken aback by the invasive feeling. I pulled away my mouth and took a breath, hoping we could try another more subtle kiss. Justin's insistent mouth pressed against mine again; I felt his hands kneading my breasts.

I pulled away again. "Thanks for dinner, Justin. I really enjoyed it, but I should get to bed. I have to get up early tomorrow for an audition."

A small scowl crossed his face. "You're not going to ask me in?"

"Sorry, no. Maybe next time—"

"Okay." He shrugged. "I'll call you soon. Good night, Gillian."

I let myself into my apartment and shut the door behind me with a sigh. It hadn't been the greatest date. Still, Justin was worth a second chance. I wasn't sure if he'd call me, but if he did I'd go out with him again.

I woke up at the crack of dawn, feeling very horny. I stretched and ran my hands over my breasts until my nipples stiffened. Justin . . . what would his mouth feel like on my nipples? He had a wonderful full-lipped mouth. . . .

I ran my hands down to my legs and caressed the sensitive skin inside my thighs. I felt wetness seeping between my legs. I closed my eyes and rubbed the folds of my vulva. Justin . . . . I tried hard to keep him in my mind, but his sleek blond hair and small features dissolved into another image . . . dark curly hair and deep brown eyes, lips and tongue that could drive me wild . . . Greg.

I took a hairbrush from my bedside table. I turned over so I was resting on my knees and shoulders. I gently stroked the hairbrush handle against my clit and moaned with pleasure. I rubbed harder and faster, remembering Greg's long, thick cock pumping in and out of my pussy. . . . I screamed so loudly I was sure I'd woken the neighbors.

I had to shower and dress hastily to make it to my audition on time. I arrived feeling tired and stressed. I was trying out for a cruise-line commercial that required an extremely perky performance. I came off like a cranky toddler on the verge of throwing the mother of all tantrums. I knew I didn't have a chance of getting the job.

I went straight home and tried to nap, but I felt too tense. I tried to think about Justin. Why didn't I long for him the way I had with David and Greg? He was perfectly nice, smart and attractive and funny. Why didn't he excite me very much?

"*You've had only one date with him,*" Miss Prudence scolded. "*Give the man a chance.*"

"*If the chemistry isn't there now, it probably never will be,*" said Miss Hornypants.

"*Sex isn't everything,*" replied Miss Prudence. "*It was with David—and look at how that turned out.*"

I felt more confused than ever. I turned over on my side, pulled the covers over my head and finally fell into a light doze.

I was awakened by the ring of my cell phone. *David . . . Greg . . . Justin,* I thought through my grogginess. It was Anita.

"So how was your date with Justin last night?" she asked.

I stifled a yawn. "Okay, I guess."

"Just okay?"

"Well, the restaurant was great, and we had a pretty good time. But I just didn't feel all that attracted to him physically. He wanted to come in after our date and seemed grouchy when I said no."

"Did you kiss him at least?"

"Yes . . . it was all right."

"So he's no David."

"He's no Greg either."

"Who's Greg?"

Oh, crap. I'd forgotten that Anita didn't know about my night with David and Greg.

"Oh, just a fellow actor I met once briefly. Very attractive guy," I said casually.

"Sounds like you're more interested in this Greg than in Justin."

"That's true. But like I said, I met this guy only once . . . don't even know his last name or whether he's unattached."

"Too bad. Well, maybe you'll run into him again sometime. Meanwhile, are you going to go out with Justin again?"

"Sure, if he calls. I'm not sure he will."

"I bet he will. He's a better prospect than Rick, that's for sure. I just came back from lunch with him. My god, what a boring guy . . . so full of shit. He spent the whole time talking about himself and his successful catering business. He kept trying to impress me, and after ten minutes I couldn't wait to get out of there."

I gave a sympathetic laugh. "Sorry, Anita. At least you can cross him off your list after one date. And maybe Lorenzo will be an improvement."

Anita let out one of her derisive snorts. "I certainly hope so. I don't see how he could be any worse."

Justin called me the next day to ask me out again. I didn't feel that wonderful rush of delight David's calls had always engendered, but I was glad he wanted to see me again.

"Why don't you come over here for dinner? I'm a pretty good cook," I suggested. I thought, *What the hell—I need to find out if we're sexually compatible. Might as well do it sooner rather than later.*

Justin seemed pleased by the invitation. "That sounds great. How about tomorrow night at seven?"

"Perfect. Now, tell me what you'd like for dinner."

"Oh, anything is fine."

"Anything? Okay, how about pan-fried liver and onions with lima beans on the side?"

A moment of horrified silence. Then he laughed. "Okay, anything but liver and lima beans."

"I have a great recipe for steak kebabs—does that sound good?"

"Sounds delicious. I'll bring some pinot noir."

"Perfect. I look forward to seeing you tomorrow night." I allowed a flirtatious note to creep into my voice. I wanted Justin to know that I had planned a memorable night.

"I *really* look forward to it," Justin replied. My message had been received.

Justin arrived promptly at seven, looking sleek and boyishly handsome. In addition to the wine, he brought me a bouquet of spring flowers and a box of éclairs from a local bakery. "You've just earned a billion brownie points," I said.

We drank the delicious pinot noir in the kitchen while I broiled the kebabs, stirred the almond pilaf and tossed the salad. He talked about his day at the office. I found myself tuning him out, but I tried to look interested and murmur appropriate comments.

My dinner turned out perfectly. I was gratified by Justin's genuine compliments. He ate two servings of everything.

"Why don't we take our dessert and coffee into the living room?" I suggested. He seemed to like that idea very much.

He sat close to me on the sofa, one thigh pressing against mine as we sipped coffee and savored the exquisite éclairs. Our conversation slowly dwindled. I felt an expectant warmth flow through my body.

"You have a smudge of cream right here. . . ." said Justin,

touching my chin. I took his hand in mine and licked the cream off his finger.

"Gillian. . . ." he breathed my name and put his arms around me. His cologne was still too strong but not as overpowering as the last time.

He crushed my mouth hard with his lips. I pushed him away. "Gentle, Justin. Slow down. We have all night. . . ."

He kissed me again with somewhat less urgency. I pulled off his jacket and unknotted his tie. His breathing was rapid and shallow. He nearly ripped off my blouse and bra. "Slow down," I reminded him again.

He grasped my breasts in his hands and kneaded them. "Gentle," I said again. I was starting to feel like a dog trainer.

I rubbed the large bulge in his pants. He dropped his hands from my breasts and leaned against the soft cushions, moaning. I got down on my knees and unbuckled his belt. "Do you want me to take your cock out?" I whispered.

"Unnnnnnnnnnnnhhhhhhhh . . ." he replied. I took that as a yes.

I unzipped his fly and released his hard cock. *Not as long or as thick as David's or Greg's, but it will do,* I thought critically.

I licked the head. "Auuuughhhh," said Justin. Apparently he liked it. I licked a few more times and then slid the shaft into my mouth. Justin grabbed my head and started pumping his cock in and out. I could feel the head banging against the roof of my mouth. After less than a minute he shouted, "Unnnn-hhhh . . . auuuughhh . . ." and spurted.

I hadn't expected it. I swallowed his cum and tried to swallow my disappointment.

Justin was lying against the pillows with his eyes closed. He looked passed out. I stood in front of him and lifted my skirt.

"Justin?"

He opened his eyes.

"I'd like to come, too."

"Oh, sure. Sorry."

"Please pull down my panties."

He yanked them down and stared at my pussy.

"I'd like you to lick me. . . ." I said seductively.

He looked uncomfortable. He flicked his tongue a few times over my lips, so lightly I could barely feel it. *At this rate it will take me three hours to come*, I thought. I took his hand and rubbed his index finger against my clit. "That's nice," I murmured. "Now use your other hand to fuck me. . . ."

He looked startled by my use of the F word, but he slid three fingers into my warm opening. "That's it," I said encouragingly. "That feels wonderful. . . . Press my clit a little harder. . . ."

I closed my eyes and rocked my hips faster. I allowed myself to fantasize about Greg again . . . his long, hard shaft and tight balls . . . I finally felt the burst of a small orgasm. I cried out softly as I convulsed around Justin's fingers.

"Thanks. That was very nice," I said formally. I pulled up my panties and dropped my skirt. I sat on the couch and snuggled against his chest. "Perhaps we could have a second round when you've had a chance to recover," I suggested.

"God, Gillian, I'm afraid not. I'm really wiped out."

"Oh. Too bad." I tried to mask the disappointment in my voice. "Well, why don't you spend the night and we could make love again in the morning?"

Justin looked doubtful for a moment. Then he glanced at the expression on my face and correctly guessed that I'd be pissed if he left.

"Okay, sure. I'll have to get up pretty early to get back to my apartment and get ready for work."

"No problem. I don't mind waking up early—and I can always go back to sleep after you've left." I was determined to make this relationship work on some level.

* * *

Justin snored. And thrashed. And stole the blankets. I had a miserable night. Every time I dozed off he would snort loudly, jab me with a sharp elbow or yank the covers off me.

At the break of dawn I woke up again when I heard him peeing in the bathroom. I lay there groggily as he slid back in bed.

"Good morning," he said cheerfully. "I slept really well last night. How about you?"

"Um, not so well. You snored and thrashed a bit." *Understatement of the year*, I thought.

"Oh, sorry about that." I felt his hard-on against my thigh. He pushed his hand between my legs. I wasn't even wet—I'd never felt less like having sex.

By closing my eyes and thinking about Greg I managed to secrete a little juice. Justin rammed his cock into me before I was ready. He pumped a few times and then came with an "unnnhhhh" and an "auughhh." He rolled off me.

"You didn't come, did you?"

"No, I didn't." I sounded petulant.

"I'm sorry. Here, let me—"

"No, no, it's okay. I don't want you to be late for work." I wanted this guy out of here as quickly as possible.

He dressed and kissed me tenderly. "Go back to sleep, darling Gillian," he said. "I'll be thinking about you. . . . I'll call you tonight."

After he left I sighed deeply. Justin could be so sweet. If only the sex were better . . . Well, perhaps I could work with him. He wasn't stupid, and he was definitely eager to please me. . . .

I finally fell back to sleep.

15

Justin and I saw each other only a few times over the next three weeks. He did work obscenely long hours, and I was performing in *Final Thoughts* six days a week.

I invited Justin, Anita and Lorenzo, Steve and Oliver to see me in the play. We went out for drinks afterward, and I reveled in the praise of my friends. "You were wonderful . . . you stole the show, Jill," said Justin. He was so proud, as if I'd just won *American Idol* or been crowned Miss Universe. I grimaced. Justin's compliment was sweet, but I *hated* to be called Jill.

Anita seemed happy in Lorenzo's company. He was a ridiculously handsome Italian shoe designer. I found him a bit smarmy and shallow—he didn't seem to have much in the brains department—but he was certainly charming and attentive to Anita. Anita said to me later, "He's good enough—for now."

"I feel the same way about Justin," I replied.

I continued to enjoy Justin's company—we always had a good time together—but our sex life improved only a little. He was uncomfortable with dirty talk and exotic positions. I tried to coax him into telling me his fantasies, but he didn't seem to have any—ones that involved me, anyway. He often came long before I was ready to climax. Still, he was anxious to please me, and I hoped that our time in bed would become more exciting and satisfying.

Our most erotic lovemaking occurred one night when we'd both had too many margaritas at the Mexican restaurant. Fortunately Justin's cock wasn't affected by the alcohol. By the time we got back to my apartment, he was rock hard. He tore at my clothes, popping buttons off my blouse. I was turned on by his urgency. He rubbed my clit—a bit too hard so I guided his hand with mine, showing him exactly how I liked to be touched.

"That's it, darling, just a little pressure . . . keep going . . . talk dirty to me. . . ."

"I . . . I like your pussy. It's always so wet and warm," he said hoarsely.

"Yes . . . and I like your cock. I like to lick it and suck it and hump it. . . ."

I moved his hand faster, increasing the friction against my clit. I felt my body shudder with a deep orgasm. "That was very nice, Justin," I cooed. "Now tell me exactly what you want me to do to you."

His face was flushed, and his eyes were bright. Still, he was hesitant and shy.

I knelt in front of him and rubbed the hard bulge in his pants. "Would you like me to take it out, Justin? Would you like me to suck your cock?"

"Yes," he replied in a faint whisper.

I unzipped his fly and pulled out his hard cock. The head was red and swollen. I flicked my tongue over it several times and then sucked hard while I stroked the shaft. Justin closed his eyes and moaned with pleasure. When I knew he was on the verge of coming, I opened my mouth and jerked him off. He groaned as his cum spurted all over my face and into my mouth.

I smiled up at him. "Now that was hot! I hope we can be even more kinky and wild."

Justin returned my smile. "I never thought of myself as kinky—but I'll do my best to get in touch with my wild side."

Aunt Mary came to the city for a visit. I invited her for dinner so she could meet Justin. "Very nice young man," she said approvingly when he was in the kitchen making coffee for us. She didn't actually say it, but her tone implied, "A much better choice than David Wentworth."

"Yes," I agreed, trying to sound enthusiastic. "He's very nice."

Caroline visited me for a weekend. When I introduced her to Justin, she was terribly impressed. "He's *sooooo cuuuute,*" she gushed.

"Cuteness is nice, but there are more important qualities in a man," I responded. I sounded like our eternally pessimistic Great-Grandma Rose.

Caroline paid no attention to me—as usual. "Do you think you'll marry him?" she asked.

"For god's sake, Caroline, I've known him only a month. Who knows what will happen?"

"Well, sooorry," humphed Caroline. "I just asked a question."

Her question may have been silly, but it made me wonder about my future with Justin. *No, I won't marry him*, I thought. *I'm never going to fall in love with Justin.*

One morning I was at Java Java with Anita, drinking lattes and idly leafing through a fashion magazine. She was reading the newspaper. I saw her stiffen suddenly.

"What is it?" I asked.

"Oh, nothing," she said too casually.

"You can't fool me. It's definitely something," I said, snatching the paper out of her hands. I immediately saw what had grabbed her attention. A small blurb in the gossip column about the lavish wedding of David Wentworth and Sandra Winthrop. I felt a sharp little sting.

"Sorry, Gillian. I didn't want you to see that."

I shrugged. "No big deal. I knew it was coming. It really doesn't matter to me. I just feel sorry for Elizabeth Stone. She must be miserable."

I flipped open the fashion magazine again, determined to push David out of my mind.

After the play's run ended, my agent Ellen sent me to an audition for a commercial. Hudson's, a Manhattan jewelry store, was advertising an engagement-ring sale. I was ecstatic when Ellen called to say I had the part. Chris Benson was slated to play my fiancé; we'd acted together before, and I liked him. I also knew the director, Joanne Wallace, and enjoyed working with her.

The day before the shoot, Ellen called to tell me that Chris Benson was in the hospital; he'd been injured in a car accident.

"Oh, my god, is it serious?" I asked.

"He'll be okay, but he has a broken leg and a concussion. So obviously he's not going to be at the shoot tomorrow. But Joanne told me they hired their second choice, so I'm sure it will be fine."

"Oh, I'm sure it will be fine, too. I just hope Chris recovers quickly."

I arrived at the shoot early and in a very good mood, although I was still concerned about Chris. Joanne and I drank coffee and chatted as the techs set up the lighting.

"I think you'll like the actor we hired," she said. "He's not as experienced as Chris, but he's very talented."

"Well, I love working with new people."

"And, speak of the devil, here he is," said Joanne. "Hey, Greg, over here, meet your costar." She waved him over.

A tall, lean young man with dark, curly hair. He smiled and waved back and then stopped short when he registered my face. *Oh, my god—it's that Greg. David's Greg. Ménage-à-trois Greg.* I swayed a little.

"Greg, this is Gillian Monroe. Gillian, this is Greg Warren."

Greg and I stared at each other speechlessly for a minute. Greg recovered first. "Nice to meet you, Gillian," he said, extending his hand.

I shook it formally. "Hi, Greg. I'm glad we'll be working together," I murmured, fighting back the blush that threatened to suffuse my face.

"Okay, we need to get you two kids in makeup and wardrobe," said Joanne briskly.

The fifteen minutes we spent in makeup gave me a chance to get my head together. Greg sat in a chair just a few feet away; I smiled at him tentatively in the big mirror as we were beautified. He smiled back. We talked casually—about Chris's accident, *Final Thoughts,* even the weather. I finally relaxed. *I can do this,* I thought. *I'll work with this guy for a few hours and then never see him again.*

Wardrobe dressed me in a long, pale pink cotton dress. It was pretty and feminine; the color and design flattered me. Greg was dressed in a simple white shirt and dark blue pants.

Greg also seemed relaxed by that point. The atmosphere was almost normal when we started working with Joanne. "Okay, as you guys know, this is a very romantic scene," she said. "Greg, you're going to propose to Gillian. Get down on one knee, give her a soulful look, and then say your line. Gillian, you're going to look incredulous for a moment. Then give us a big, joyful smile and say your line. Greg, you stand and slide the ring on her finger and give her a big kiss—make it as passionate as possible. Think of those romance-novel covers with Fabio and those busty chicks."

I swallowed hard. *This might not be as easy as I thought it would be.*

"Okay, let's do a quick run-through," said Joanne.

Greg dropped to one knee and gazed up at me. Those chestnut-brown eyes fringed with long black lashes . . . I'd forgotten how they mesmerized me.

Greg said his line. I was so distracted I completed blanked on mine. I looked at Joanne helplessly.

"Yes, darling, I'll marry you," prompted Joanne.

I repeated the line; it sounded incredibly flat. Greg rose from his knees and slipped the ring on my left hand. I stood stiffly as he embraced me and gave me a quick kiss.

"Okay," said Joanne, trying to keep the exasperation out of her voice. "That's not exactly what I had in mind. We need a little more passion. In fact, a lot more passion. Greg, you need to give her a much bigger kiss. And, Gillian, don't just stand there—put your arms around his neck. Remember, you're madly in love with this guy, and today is the happiest day of your life."

I blushed hotly. I was embarrassed by my poor performance and embarrassed at the idea of acting passionate with Greg.

We tried three more times. Each time was worse than the last. I saw the ad-agency executive whispering furiously to Joanne; she whispered back. *Oh, god, am I going to lose this job?* I thought frantically.

Joanne turned back to us with a forced smile. "Okay, kids. You're obviously not comfortable with each other. So let's take a twenty-minute break. You two go out for coffee, go for a walk, whatever . . . just try to get relaxed."

"That sounds like a good idea," I said with relief. I turned to Greg. "It's pretty nice outside. Is a walk okay with you?"

"Sure, that's fine."

It was a glorious late April day, with a soft breeze pushing puffy clouds across the Easter–egg blue sky. Greg and I walked down the street to a small park. Drifts of pink blossoms floated from the trees and swirled across our path. "Gillian, do you want to sit here?" Greg asked, indicating a bench.

"Good idea."

We sat several feet apart. Greg broke the silence by saying, "So this is a little awkward."

I had to laugh. "Awkward doesn't even begin to describe it. I guess we should have known we might run into each other."

Greg stretched out his long legs and leaned against the bench back. "The idea did occur to me. But my agent said I'd be working today with an actress named Jill—I didn't guess that it would be you."

"And I thought I would be working with Chris . . . didn't know until yesterday that he'd been replaced." Another minute of silence. Finally I said, "As you probably know, David just got married."

"I heard about that." Greg turned to look at me with a question in his eyes.

"The answer is yes, I was very upset and angry when I found out about Sandra. I had no idea he was seriously involved with another woman. I broke it off immediately. I haven't seen him for months."

"Neither have I," said Greg with a grimace. "After that night . . . well, the next time I saw him at the gym, he was pissed at me. I didn't give a crap. I quit my personal-trainer job the following week."

"I see," I said, wishing I could think of a better response.

Greg started to jiggle his left leg, a nervous tic I remembered well. "Gillian . . . I do want to apologize to you for running out that night. I did really . . . enjoy it with you. I just felt . . . weird about the whole thing. For a while I completely forgot David was there. And then when I remembered—it just kind of freaked me out."

"Don't apologize . . . I understand." I hesitated. "It was weird for me, too. I'd never done anything like that before. David was persuasive."

Greg gave me a wry smile. "I know all about David's powers of persuasion. I'd never done anything like that, either, but he convinced me."

I smiled back. "The truth is, I'm glad it's over with David."

"The truth is, David is a manipulative, selfish son of a bitch. Let's make a deal: we'll never talk about him again. Okay?"

"Deal." I held out my hand. Greg gave it shake but didn't release it. He entwined his strong, warm fingers with mine. I felt my heartbeat accelerate.

"Gillian . . ." Greg scooted closer to me. "I think it would be a good idea for us to practice before we go back to the studio."

"Practice?" The word came out as a whisper.

"Yes . . . like this." Greg bent down and kissed me, softly at first and then with increasing pressure. My nipples hardened immediately, and I felt a warm, glowing sensation between my legs. If my mouth had been free I would have blurted out, "I want you so much."

I wrapped my arms around him and caressed the nape of his neck. The smell of sun-ripened tomatoes . . .

Greg finally pulled away, leaving me breathless. He ran his thumb over my swollen lips. "Time to get back to work, Gillian."

We did two more run-throughs; Joanne was pleased with our performances. "What did you two do, make out for twenty minutes?" she joked. Greg and I exchanged secret smiles.

"Okay, let's shoot it," Joanne said.

This time Greg's voice was a little strained with emotion when he delivered his proposal. My voice trembled a bit when I responded. As he slipped the ring on my finger, my hand shook slightly. He wrapped his arms around me, and I lifted my face to accept his kiss. I felt my nipples stiffen as his warm lips pressed against mine. I wanted to stay in his embrace forever.

Joanne yelled, "Cut," and I was yanked back to reality. "I think that's it," said Joanne. "You guys really nailed it." The advertising executive looked like he'd swoon with relief.

I was back in my own clothes, back in my ordinary world. I lingered, looking around for Greg, but he seemed to have disappeared. I said good-bye to Joanne and headed for the exit.

I was just opening the door when Greg intercepted me and offered to walk me to the subway station. I felt a tingle of excitement. Perhaps he didn't want to say good-bye any more than I did.

We talked easily during the five-minute walk to the station. I was so aware of his closeness—I wanted so badly to hold his hand or slip my arm around his waist.

"Well, here you are," Greg said as we loitered outside the subway entrance. "It was great to work with you, Gillian. And I'm glad we had that little talk about . . . you know who and you know what."

I laughed at his careful evasion. "I'm glad, too."

He hesitated. I looked straight into his eyes. *Please, please, please ask me for my number*, I thought desperately.

"Well, take care, Gillian," he said and turned away. I stood there and stared at his retreating back, feeling as if my soul had been crushed.

During the subway ride home I tried to downplay my feelings. *You still barely know the guy—and you probably won't see him again. He must have a girlfriend—a guy like that wouldn't stay unattached for long. Why would he ever be interested in you, anyway? He was nice to you but probably thinks you're some kind of nympho . . .*

As hard as I tried, I couldn't soothe my wounded heart. I

wanted Greg, wanted him more than I had ever wanted anyone—even David. It was so much more than a physical attraction. I felt a deep connection to this man. Misery washed over me as I acknowledged the truth: I had fallen for someone I could never have.

16

Over the next few weeks I tried hard to forget about Greg. Erasing David from my mind had been a picnic in comparison. Spending time with Justin seemed to be the easiest way to distract myself.

Sex with Justin gradually improved but still wasn't even close to the earth-shaking experiences I'd had with David and Greg. Justin could almost always make me come but never with the intensity and frequency I'd known before. I often felt a mild discontent, a simmering frustration in the background of my psyche.

One morning I woke up early and decided to surprise him. As he slept peacefully, I pulled the covers down and started licking his balls and shaft. I watched as his shaft stiffened and lengthened. When he was fully awake—and fully hard—I straddled his hips and rubbed the head of his cock against my lips and clit, making myself hot and wet. I slid his cock into my pussy and rode him hard, squeezing his shaft with my muscles. "Christ, that's good," he moaned. We both came intensely. Satisfied and sleepy, we snuggled together in bed. This was my favorite part with Justin; he was always very tender. It was a wonderful change from David's postcoital distance.

He stroked my hair and gazed into my eyes. "Jill?"

"I should have told you this before, Justin . . . I really don't like nicknames. Please call me Gillian."

"Okay, Gillian. I've been thinking . . . we've been together a while now, and things are going so well. Perhaps it's time to take things to the next level."

I lowered my gaze and shifted uncomfortably under the sheets. "What do you mean?"

He dropped a kiss on my collarbone. "Well, I thought you could move in with me."

I was horrified. I'd been to Justin's Lexington Avenue studio just a few times. The high-rise building was great, but the apartment was dark and cramped. Justin was a bit of a slob. The place often smelled like sour milk or leftover pizza. The idea of giving up my lovely brownstone apartment for his cave was appalling.

I used every ounce of my acting talent to conceal my dismay. "Justin, that's so sweet of you to ask . . . but I really like this apartment."

"Well, okay, I could move in here with you when my lease expires."

I evaded his gaze. "Justin . . . if you want to know the truth, I don't feel ready for this step. Maybe I'll feel differently in a few months—"

Justin pulled away from me and flung the comforter aside. He was pissed.

"Don't try to pacify me with false promises, Gillian. I'm falling in love with you. But you're not even here—not really with me—most of the time."

"I don't know what you mean." I'd never seen Justin angry before; I didn't know how to handle it.

"Yes, you know what I mean." He started yanking on his

clothes. "I think there must be someone else—you're preoccupied with another man."

I gave him an imploring look. "You know I've been faithful to you—"

"Physically maybe. But you're always thinking about someone else." He shoved his feet into his loafers.

I didn't know how to respond. I stared at the floor.

"Look at me, Gillian." His tone was so harsh; he seemed like a stranger.

I raised my eyes.

"I want truthful answers. Do you love me?"

"No," I whispered.

"Will you ever love me?"

I wanted so badly to give him the answer he needed. But I couldn't. "No. I'm sorry, Justin."

"Well, then, that's that." Justin's tone was brusque, but I could hear the pain in his voice.

"Justin, I wish I could—"

He didn't want to listen. He stormed out of the bedroom. When I heard the front door slam behind him, I burst into tears.

I called Anita, and she came over for another rescue operation. She made chamomile tea to soothe my frazzled nerves. I sipped it as I slumped at the kitchen table.

"Well, you always said Justin was good enough for now," she said. "You never intended to get seriously involved with him."

I ran my hand through my tangled hair. "I know. But I feel like such a jerk for breaking his heart. I had no idea he felt so strongly about me."

"What could you do? Pretending to care deeply about him would have been much worse. The poor guy would have been convinced you had a future together."

"I know, I know. Still . . . I wish I could make things better for him somehow."

Anita touched my hand. "The best thing would be to just let him go. He's very attractive . . . he'll find the right woman."

I gave her half a smile. "You really should write an advice column after you give up modeling."

Anita rolled her eyes. "That could be any day now. It's getting harder to compete with these anorexic fourteen-year-olds. Sometimes I feel ancient."

"You get more beautiful every year. Speaking of beauties . . . how's Lorenzo these days?"

"Oh, fine. We're still having a good time together. I don't have to worry about him falling hard for me—he's too much in love with himself."

I laughed and felt almost human again.

I sent Justin a short note of apology. He never responded.

I did miss him, far more than I had expected. I was tempted to call him and make up, but I knew that would be too cruel and selfish. I'd experienced enough romantic pain over the past year—I didn't want to inflict it on anyone else.

Joanne Wallace called to invite me to a party. "Chris Benson is still recovering from his accident, but he's doing well. I invited him and his wife, a couple of other people. I thought you'd like to join us."

"That's so nice, Joanne. I'll bring some crab dip and pita chips."

I'd been lonely the past few weeks without Justin. Anita had been traveling a lot for various jobs, and Steve was vacationing in Europe with Oliver. I'd gone out with Natalie a few times, but I found her hyper personality exhausting. I needed some new company. I arrived at Joanne's apartment feeling buoyant.

Joanne's partner, Heather, answered the door, and I handed

her the dip and chips. I saw Chris sitting in an armchair with his crutches by his side. A cast covered his right leg from thigh to ankle. "Chris, you poor baby!" I said, kissing his cheek. "How are you coping?"

Chris gave me his crooked smile, "Pretty well. My leg hurt like a bitch after the accident, but I'm lucky I wasn't hurt more seriously. This stupid sixteen-year-old hit me head-on."

"Well, I'm sorry you lost the jewelry store commercial because of the accident."

"Yeah, I wasn't too happy about that. But Joanne told me the guy who replaced me did a decent job—eventually."

I laughed nervously. "It took a while for us to get comfortable with each other, but, yes, I think it turned out pretty well."

I turned to greet Nancy, his wife, and commiserated with her about Chris's misfortune. "He's driving me up the wall," she confided in a whisper. "Having him home all day while I'm trying to write is making me crazy."

"I can imagine," I whispered back. "Tell you what, I'll come over some afternoons and entertain him. I know he likes chess and backgammon. I'll bring my sets over."

"God bless you," Nancy said fervently.

There were about a dozen other guests at the party, mostly people I knew from work. I hadn't seen many of them in quite a while; it was great to catch up.

Heather opened the front door for two more guests. A tall, dark young man. I swallowed hard—*Greg.* And a woman. A stunning strawberry blonde with gray-blue eyes and adorable freckles across her nose. I felt a plunging sensation in my stomach.

My eyes met Greg's, and he froze. "Oh, hi, Gillian," he said a moment later. "Good to see you."

I gave him a tense smile. "Hi, Greg, so glad we ran into each other again."

"Let me introduce you to Sophie." He put a hand on the beautiful woman's arm. "Sophie Gervais, this is Gillian Monroe."

"Hello, Gillian," she said with a charming French accent.

"Sophie is in New York for six months. She's studying fashion design," said Greg.

"Oh, of course. I love your outfit—that dress is stunning," I gushed. "And those silver earrings are wonderful. So unique." My performance sounded insincere even to my ears.

"Thank you," replied Sophie, giving me a blindingly white smile. We chatted a bit. She was from Paris—of course. Beautiful, smart, sophisticated, charismatic—I thought my head would explode with jealousy.

Greg stood there awkwardly, watching us converse. He offered to get us drinks. I declined, and Sophie requested white wine. Greg set off for the kitchen.

I chatted with Sophie for a few more minutes; under other circumstances I would have liked her a lot. I murmured an excuse and drifted away. I locked myself in the bathroom and sat on the toilet lid, biting my knuckles in frustration and pain. I couldn't stand to see Greg with another woman—especially a woman like Sophie.

I took a few long, deep breaths and returned to the party. I tracked down Joanne and thanked her for a lovely time.

"You're not leaving already?"

"Sorry. I'm not feeling well . . . I think I'm coming down with a cold or something."

A deep voice behind me said, "Sorry to hear that, Gillian."

I turned to find Greg standing inches away, staring down at me. He pressed a cool palm against my forehead. "You do feel a little warm. You should drink lots of juice and stay in bed tomorrow."

I gave him a very small smile. "That sounds like a great idea."

"I wish we'd had more time to talk . . . but perhaps we'll see each other again soon."

"I hope so." I noticed that Joanne was watching us very intently.

"Well, I should be going . . . thanks again, Joanne. Good to see you, Greg." I waved to Chris across the room. "Take care—I promise I'll come over to visit and play chess." I managed to sound cheerful and casual—as if I had absolutely nothing on my mind.

Back at my apartment, I had a good long cry in the shower. *Why, why, why?* I moaned to myself. *Why didn't I meet Greg earlier and under other circumstances—at an audition or a party—before my disastrous affair with David and my fling with Justin?* I wiped my tear-stained face with a washcloth. *Fate is just too cruel*, I added melodramatically.

I slept badly and woke up the next morning with a sore throat and pounding headache. I was burning up. I checked my temperature—the thermometer read 102 degrees. I remembered something cranky Great-Grandma Rose used to say: "If you are untruthful, your lies might come true—and bite you in the ass." The little white lie I'd told the night before was taking a big chomp out of my butt.

I dragged myself to the corner store and loaded up on ibuprofen and orange juice. I tried to read, but my throbbing head made it impossible to concentrate. Even watching TV seemed to require too much effort. I tried to sleep, but by that point I couldn't stop coughing and sneezing.

I desperately needed a friend's TLC, but no one was available. Anita was shooting a magazine spread in Miami. Steve and Oliver wouldn't return from Europe until the following week. Natalie was at work. I didn't want to impose on Joanne and Heather or Chris and Nancy—they were good friends but not that close. I couldn't ask Aunt Mary to come all the way to the city to take care of me. I was so desperate I thought about calling Justin but immediately told myself it was out of the question.

I'll just have to suffer through this alone, I thought miserably. I gulped down some heavy-duty cough syrup and finally slept for a few hours.

I was awakened by the buzz of the intercom. *Who on earth could that be?* I wondered. I stumbled to the intercom and pressed the button.

"Yes?" I croaked.

"Gillian, it's Greg. Sorry to stop by unexpectedly. I just wanted to see how you're doing."

"Greg?" It seemed so surreal—I wondered if I was having a feverish dream.

"Do you mind if I come up? I've brought you some soup."

"Oh, sure, come on up."

I buzzed him through the lobby door and immediately panicked. I glanced at myself in the hallway mirror and barely recognized the wretched creature who looked back.

I rushed to the bathroom and flung on a blue terry-cloth robe. I ripped a brush through my tangled hair and rubbed a wet towel over my face. I heard a knock on the door—*damn*. I swigged some mouthwash while I spritzed myself with cologne. Another knock, louder this time. I ran to the door and opened it.

There was Greg holding a container of soup in one hand and a bouquet of red and yellow tulips in the other. I had a sudden flashback to childhood: playing "Mystery Date" with Anita and opening the little door to find the picture of the dreamboat.

"Greg, this is a nice surprise." My voice sounded raw.

"Sorry again for not calling—but I don't have your number. I made some chicken soup this afternoon, and I thought it might make you feel a little better."

I took the soup and tulips from him. "You *made* this soup?"

"Yeah, I like to cook. My mom is an amazing cook, and she

believes guys need to know their way around a kitchen. So she started teaching me and my brother at a very young age."

"That's great. And the tulips are so nice . . . thanks."

"You're welcome." Our eyes met briefly, and we both quickly looked away.

"Please come in and have a beer or something."

"No, I don't want to impose on you—I know you feel lousy—"

"No imposition. I've been dying for some company."

"Well, if you're sure it's okay . . ."

"It's more than okay." I felt a huge sneeze tickling my sinuses. "Excuse me." I grabbed a wad of tissue just in time. I sneezed like an elephant with hay fever. I blew my nose as delicately as possible, but it was difficult to be ladylike.

"Poor Gillian," said Greg sympathetically. He touched my cheek, and I nearly collapsed in his arms. Instead I pulled away slightly.

"Be careful, Greg. I don't want you catching this god-awful disease."

He grinned. "I'll take my chances."

We sat at the kitchen table and ate his soup with toasted slices of sourdough bread. "This is so good, the best chicken soup I've ever had," I said without the slightest exaggeration. "I haven't eaten all day. All of a sudden I'm starving."

"Well, that's a very good sign. Maybe you just have a twenty-four hour bug. But if you feel rotten again tomorrow, you really should see your doctor."

His sweet bossiness made me smile.

I wanted to bring up Sophie, but I was afraid it would ruin the easy camaraderie that existed between us. The last thing I wanted was to hear Greg raving about another woman. I kept expecting him to mention her name and was relieved when he didn't.

After our soup and toast dinner we watched a comically awful sci-fi/action movie on TV. We had a blast making fun of the terrible script and inept acting. "I actually tried out for the lead role in this movie a couple of years ago when I lived in LA," said Greg. "I had a couple of callbacks and was so disappointed when I didn't get the part. Now I know I had a lucky escape."

"Yeah, it's not something you'd want to add to your résumé." We smiled at each other, both remembering the lousy parts we had won and lost.

"Hey, look, it's our commercial," said Greg, leaning forward intently.

I stared at the screen. A closeup of a young, attractive couple. He falls to one knee and says, "Will you marry me, darling?" She looks like every dream she's ever had has suddenly come true. When she says yes, he rises and slips the ring on her finger. She slides into his embrace as if she's done it a million times before. They kiss for a long time. A man's honey-smooth voice says, "Hudson's. Where you'll find the right ring for the right woman."

Greg turned to me. "It came out pretty well, don't you think?"

"Oh, yes, I'm pleased with it." I stared at my teacup.

Greg picked at the label on his Heineken bottle. "Well, I should go. You need your sleep. Hope you feel better, Gillian."

We stood simultaneously, surrounded by an awkward atmosphere. "Thanks, Greg. The soup, the flowers, the company . . . it was so nice of you."

Greg touched my shoulder. "No problem. I'll check in with you in a couple of days . . . if that's okay with you."

"Of course. Let me give you my cell number."

I wrote it down on a scrap of paper, which he tucked into his jacket pocket. I walked him to the front door. "Good night, Greg."

"Good night, Gillian." He gave me one more smile and was gone.

I leaned against the door with my eyes closed, trying to beat down the fluttering hope in my chest. "Don't make too much of this," I whispered to myself sternly. "He's just being friendly. Remember Sophie. . . ."

17

I felt almost healthy the next morning. My nose had stopped running, and my fever had cooled a few degrees. I credited Greg's chicken soup—and the pleasure of his company—for this miraculous cure.

It was impossible to suppress my optimism. All through the following day I had fantasies of Greg bursting through my front door, swooping me up in his arms and declaring his undying love. *Shooting that engagement-ring commercial must have infected me with a serious strain of romanticism,* I thought wryly. Still, the developing friendship with Greg was real enough. I was so relieved—and amazed—that we'd managed to move beyond the awkward memory of that night with David.

If only the insanely perfect Sophie would haul her ass back to Paris . . . maybe I could have a chance with him, I thought wistfully. Miss Prudence popped up to scold me. "*This 'what if' and 'if only' mindset isn't going to change anything. Deal with reality, the way things really are.*"

Of course Miss P.'s advice was dead on—but could I deal with the reality of Greg's romantic involvement with Sophie?

Just the thought of him touching her . . . kissing her . . . oh, God, making love with her . . . I ground my teeth. Maybe even the most superficial friendship with Greg would be too unbearable.

Still, my heart leaped when my cell phone rang. *Please be Greg. . . .*

It was Anita, back a day early from Miami. "Oh, it's you," I said, unable to disguise my disappointment.

"Geez, don't get too excited."

"Sorry. I've been sick. I'm just getting over some horrible bug."

"Really? I know something nasty has been going around. I'm glad you're feeling better."

"How was Miami?"

"Hot and humid. I had to spend hours on the beach in the most hideous bathing suits you've ever seen. Thank god I'm getting paid a ton of money for that job."

I let out a bark of laughter. "Yeah, enough money can ease the pain of the worst job."

"So, you want to get together tonight?"

I hesitated. It would be great to see Anita, but I was still hoping Greg would call or come by. And I didn't feel like sharing the secret of my feelings for Greg at this point.

"I'd love to, Anita, but I think I should go to bed early . . . make sure I've really licked this bug."

"Okay, sure, I understand. Why don't I give you a call tomorrow. Maybe by then you'll be up for some company."

I felt a twinge of guilt, knowing I'd be more than able to cope with Greg's company. I told Anita I'd definitely see her the next day.

I was drifting off to sleep when my cell phone rang again. I flipped it open and mumbled, "Hello?"

"Hi, Gillian. I hope I didn't wake you up."

Greg. Adrenaline shot through my body.

"No, no, it's fine, I was awake," I said, sitting upright. I clutched the phone more tightly, as if it would bring Greg closer.

"How do you feel?"

"Almost back to normal. That chicken soup cured me, I'm sure of it."

His laughter was so easy and open. "I'd like to take credit for your recovery, but I think it's a bit of a stretch."

"Seriously, your company made me feel so much better." I nearly bit my tongue; I was being way too flirtatious with a man who had no romantic interest in me.

"Well, I'm glad to hear that. I'm leaving for Cape Cod tomorrow to visit my mother. I'll be gone for a week, so I just wanted to check in with you before I go."

"Oh. That should be a nice trip." A whole week—it seemed like an eternity. I desperately wanted to ask him if he was taking Sophie along.

"Yeah, I'm looking forward to a little break. So I'll talk to you when I get back."

"Have a wonderful time."

"Thanks. Take care, Gillian."

The conversation ended too quickly, leaving me with a sense of deep disappointment. *Face it, Gillian,* I thought grimly, *this guy wants a casual friendship, nothing more.*

Anita came over the following afternoon. She handed me a small present from Miami, a woven jewelry box studded with delicate shells. I covered a spike of guilt by thanking her profusely. "Hey, it's just a trinket. I didn't hide a diamond tennis bracelet inside," she joked.

I had baked brownies and made jasmine tea. "My appetite is back," I said, brushing chocolate crumbs from my mouth. "That's the one good thing about being sick—you can lose a few pounds easily. Of course, I always pack it back on once I've recovered, usually with a couple of extra pounds."

Anita nibbled at a scrap of brownie. "I felt like a tub of lard in those hideous swimsuits. They were so revealing in the most unflattering ways. My ass was hanging out, and my tits were squashed flat."

"Maybe ugly swimwear will be all the rage this summer. You and I will look like goddesses in our old suits."

"Wouldn't that be nice. Anyway, I'm sorry I wasn't around while you were sick. I know that being alone seems to magnify the misery."

"Actually a friend did stop by. He brought some homemade chicken soup."

Anita's eyebrows shot up. "He who? Steve or Oliver?"

I just *had* to say his name—I was like a thirteen-year-old with a crush on her teacher. "No, Greg Warren. I think I told you about him . . . an actor I met a while ago. We did the engagement-ring commercial together."

"Oh, right . . . the guy you found so attractive."

I nipped her speculation in the bud. "Nothing's going to happen with him. I saw him last week at a party hosted by Joanne and Heather. He was with this gorgeous French girl—Sophie or Marie or something."

"So? I've known a lot of gorgeous French women. She's not necessarily his dream girl."

"He seemed very into her. Anyway, he's just a friend."

Anita gave me a long, hard look. "If you say so."

I quickly changed the subject. "So have you seen Lorenzo recently?"

"No. He seems to be getting bored with me. I'm definitely bored with him. I think it's time for fresh meat. Are you ready for the hunt, Gillian?"

* * *

I wasn't ready for the hunt. I wasn't even interested in the hunt. I just wanted to moon over Greg.

I was horny all the time, it felt like I hadn't had sex in years. Greg starred in all my erotic fantasies. Every morning I would wake up and imagine him in bed next to me. He'd roll over and crush me to his chest. I would run my hands down his shoulders to his back and then to his ass. He would cover my throat and breasts with urgent kisses while I caressed his smooth cheeks. I'd slowly skim my fingers down the crack of his ass to his tight balls. He would take my stiff nipples—first one and then the other—into his mouth and suck gently. I'd wrap my hand around his shaft and rub the head against my pussy lips—gently at first and then with increasing pressure. I'd lie back and spread my legs, revealing myself to him without any shyness or shame. He'd slowly open my lips to stare at my pink clit. He'd flick his tongue over it just a few times, making me moan and writhe. Then he'd rub the head of his cock against my clit, pushing me to the brink. I'd beg him to make me come. He'd plunge into me, fucking me hard and deep. And we'd explode at the same time, lost in the pleasure of our bodies. . . .

My fantasies about Greg made me come so intensely I'd nearly pass out. I'd close my eyes and lie still until my heartbeat slowed and the sweat on my face dried. And I'd struggle through a moment of despair, wondering if I'd ever experience so much pleasure again with a man.

I baked another batch of brownies and took them over to Chris and Nancy's. I brought my chess set with me; Nancy thanked me again for entertaining Chris, who was going out of his mind with boredom. I wondered if I should just give up sex and devote my life to good works. It seemed like a better way to find satisfaction.

I easily beat Chris at chess, and he demanded a rematch. He was more focused during the second game and narrowly beat me. "Best of three," he insisted. We were setting up for the third game when Nancy ushered Joanne into the room. "Another visitor for you, Chris," Nancy said. "We're going to have to set up a schedule. I'll brew more coffee."

"Hi, Jo, I saw the commercial the other night, and I thought it was great," I said.

"I'm pleased with it, too. Of course it would have been better with Chris." She winked at him.

"Oh, I don't know," said Chris. "I've seen the commercial a few times—that Greg guy was pretty good. I think he and Gillian had great chemistry. It was easy to believe they were really in love."

A knife in my heart. "Of course we barely knew each other. But we did a little something called acting," I joked.

"No, I think Chris is right, you two had something unique, a rare kind of connection," said Joanne. She gave me a penetrating look, Anita could have learned a thing or two from her.

That's right, just plunge the knife deeper and twist it slowly. I shrugged nonchalantly. "Well, sometimes you can develop a rapport quickly. Of course, it's just temporary—once the job is over, so is the connection. Now, Chris, are we going to play, or have you wimped out?"

Joanne watched us play. My concentration was broken, and Chris beat me easily. Nancy invited us to stay to dinner. Joanne accepted, but I made a weak excuse and fled back to my apartment. It seemed like the world was conspiring against me—there was no respite from my fantasies about Greg.

18

The following weekend Anita persuaded me to go with her to a club opening. The pounding music and flashing lights gave me an intense headache. "I think I'm getting too old for this kind of scene," I shrieked into Anita's ear.

"Me, too," she shrieked back. "Let's get out of here. I heard about a classy new bar just a few blocks from here."

After wandering the streets for half an hour we finally found the place—Montague's. We stood in the vestibule and saw that it was indeed very classy—dark paneled walls, burgundy velvet curtains, low-murmured conversations. "It looks like a funeral home," I whispered to Anita. "And I feel ridiculous in this outfit. A purple miniskirt doesn't seem like proper attire."

"Oh, come on, don't be such a pessimist. We're here, so let's give it a try," replied Anita. She dragged me to a corner table. We ordered the cheapest white wine—$15 a glass. I cringed. My bank account was healthy these days but not that robust.

Within five minutes a coterie of Anita's admirers were vying for her attention. She seemed particularly interested in a guy named Miles who had silvery hair and a killer English accent. I watched their mating dance and tried not to let my boredom show.

Another guy named Donald seemed to give up on Anita and turned his attention to me. He was attractive and seemed nice enough, but he was way too old—and divorced, which always made me nervous. He reminded me of my dad. When Donald pulled photos of his new granddaughter out of his wallet, I knew he could never be right for me. I politely declined when he asked me to have dinner with him. I felt relieved when he made a lame excuse and wandered away.

Anita and I primped in the ladies' room. I told her I was tired and wanted to go home. "I'll just grab a cab. You can stay here with Miles. He seems like a guy with great potential. Go for it."

As soon as I got home I kicked off my shoes and flopped into bed. I slept fitfully and woke up at the crack of dawn. I dragged my ass into the shower. As I ran my soapy hands over my breasts my nipples hardened. My thoughts turned again to Greg, and the familiar longing possessed my body. I released the showerhead from the bracket and directed a warm stream of water at my pussy. I closed my eyes and leaned against the wet tiles, allowing the water to massage my lips and vulva. I spread my lips wide with one hand and aimed the stream at my clit. I moaned as my body slowly dissolved in a sea of pleasure. I slid three fingers in and out of my pussy and groaned Greg's name as I climaxed.

It felt so good to come, but I ended up more frustrated and depressed than ever. I wondered if I should have settled for Donald—he looked like a man who would know what to do in bed. One night with him might have given me some relief.

I decided to go for a jog. I ran into Natalie in the hallway; she was on her way to work. She'd been upset when she'd heard about my breakup with Justin, she seemed to take it as a personal affront.

"Gillian, I have a great new guy for you," she gushed. "His name is Bob Smith. An accountant with one of the big mid-town firms—"

I cut her off. "Thanks for thinking of me, Natalie, but at the moment I'm not really looking for someone. I've put my love life on hold."

Natalie looked incredulous. "You can't be too picky, Gillian. I mean, one of these days you'll wake up and you'll be twenty-nine and still single." She made it sound like a fate worse than death.

It was hard not to laugh. "I appreciate your concern. But I think I'll find the right guy . . . when the time is right."

"Okay." Natalie shrugged. "I have to rush, I'm late already. See ya." She flew through the front door.

An accountant named Bob Smith. Just that much info and I'm bored with him, I thought wryly.

I was paying bills and catching up with e-mail when my cell rang. It was Anita, ready to give me a review of the previous evening. She'd gone out for dinner with Miles and planned to see him again. "It's so nice to spend time with a *mature* man," she said.

"Just how *mature* is he, anyway?"

"Forty-nine."

"Nearly twice your age."

"It doesn't bother me. Going out with a distinguished gentleman beats the hell out of dating immature little twerps. He's smart and sophisticated. He's here for only a few months on a consulting job; then he's going back to London. But London isn't too far away. . . ." Anita sounded excited about this budding romance.

"Well, if you feel comfortable with him, I guess the age difference doesn't matter. Call me after your next date. Let's hope he doesn't need Viagra to perform."

Anita laughed. "Something tells me his performance will be all natural—and magnificent."

After we hung up I focused again on my e-mail. When the phone rang again I assumed it was Anita calling with another tidbit about Miles.

"Hey, Gillian, how are you?"

Greg's warm, friendly voice. My bones seemed to melt.

"Great. Are you back from the Cape?"

"Yes. I had a really good time with my mom and some old friends. I thought about you. You would have enjoyed it."

I was startled. How to interpret that comment? "Was Sophie with you?" I blurted out. I wanted to slap myself.

"Sophie? No. I broke up with her a few weeks ago."

It was the last thing I'd expected him to say. "Really? She seemed very nice . . . and of course she was gorgeous. . . ."

"True. But for some reason . . ." He hesitated, trying to find the right words. "For some reason I didn't feel a connection with her. We always had a good time together, but something was missing."

I closed my eyes in bliss. "I know what you mean. I dated a guy named Justin for a few months. He was smart, attractive, nice . . . there was absolutely nothing wrong with him . . . but I just didn't feel a connection. I had to break it off. He was very upset. I felt like a bitch, but I just couldn't let it go on."

"Hey, maybe we should set up Justin with Sophie," he joked.

I laughed. "That's my neighbor Natalie's job. She won't be happy until everyone in Manhattan is coupled."

"Okay, I don't want to step on Natalie's toes. We'll let her handle it."

A brief pause. I felt my heart racing.

"Gillian—"

"Greg—"

Our words collided. "Go ahead," I said.

"Well, it's such a nice day. I thought maybe we could have a picnic lunch in Central Park. If you're not busy or anything," he added hastily.

His nervousness was adorable. "That sounds wonderful. I'd love to have a picnic with you."

He agreed to make sandwiches; I said I'd bring fruit, cookies and drinks. We decided to rendezvous at noon.

As I packed my tote bag I felt deliriously happy, like a Disney heroine ready to break into song and dance. I rushed to our meeting place, arriving fifteen minutes early. I waited anxiously as I scanned the passing pedestrians. Finally a tall, familiar figure strode down the sidewalk toward me.

"Gillian." He smiled at me, and I wanted to fling my arms around his neck.

It was a gorgeous early summer day, but it was midweek so the park wasn't too crowded. We found a spot under the branches of a huge oak tree. Greg pulled a red plaid blanket from his backpack and spread it on the grass. We flopped down and set up our picnic.

I devoured two huge sandwiches bulging with rare roast beef and boursin cheese. "This bread is great—where did you get it?" I asked.

"I baked it myself."

"You're kidding! You really are a talented chef."

"Thanks. Years ago I did seriously consider cooking as a career. But my cousin Marc discouraged me from pursuing it. He's the chef/owner of a fantastic Italian restaurant in Boston's North End. He loves it—but it's his whole life. No room or time for anything else. I don't have that workaholic quality."

"Thank god for that. Workaholics can be pretty boring. I like to cook, too. I think I'm pretty good, but I'm not nearly as talented as you are."

Greg gave me his devastating smile. "I'd be glad to teach you a few things . . . techniques and tricks I picked up from Marc and my mother."

"I'd love that." I felt a little shimmer run through my body. Just the thought of spending more time with Greg—just the idea of his proximity—was enough to thrill me.

We followed the sandwiches with dessert. Greg complimented me on my chocolate-chunk pecan cookies. We stretched out on the blanket; I released a sigh of contentment. I looked over at Greg. His eyes were closed.

"Are you asleep?"

"Yes, deeply asleep." He opened one eye and smiled at me.

I laughed. "It's strange, Greg. I feel so comfortable with you—but I actually know very little about you."

"What do you want to know?"

I propped myself up on one elbow. "Well, where are you from?"

"Boston originally. My dad was a cop. He died suddenly when I was ten—a heart attack while pursuing a bank-robbery suspect through Boston Common. My mom was devastated. She decided she didn't want to raise kids in the city, so she moved us to Cape Cod. She had a sister there. Aunt Louise helped take care of me and Ryan—my younger brother—while Mom worked. Money was pretty tight, and of course we missed Dad so much, but I had a pretty good childhood."

"I'm so sorry about your dad. It must have been a shock to lose him that way. How did you get into acting?"

"Oh, I always loved movies and plays. I joined the theater club in high school. I never intended to make it my career—like I said, I was interested in becoming a chef. Or maybe a professional baseball player. I pitched for a Cape league team one summer. I had a blast, but I knew I wasn't talented enough for the big league. Then I saw my cousin Marc going through hell during his early years as a chef, and I ruled that career out. So I thought I'd try my hand at acting. It's been a struggle, but I'm finally getting somewhere."

"God, tell me about it. It's taken me nearly six years just to climb out of poverty." I told him about growing up with Anita in Hanover. "We couldn't wait to get out of that small town, but now we enjoy going back to visit. I guess you can't appreciate the simple life until you've had a taste of the complicated life."

"I know exactly what you mean. When I was a teenager all I wanted to do was move to a big city—New York or LA, maybe Chicago. Boston seemed too tame to me. But now I enjoy all the pleasures of my hometown. . . ." His voice trailed off. He looked directly into my eyes. My lips parted in anticipation. "Gillian. . . ."

I leaned forward, and my mouth met his. So warm, so soft. He lifted his right hand and caressed my cheek. The kiss deepened and intensified. I felt his tongue slide between my lips and engage my tongue. I wrapped my arms around him and pulled him down on top of me. I wanted to feel the entire length of his body pressing against me.

We kissed and kissed. I felt a warm wetness trickling between my thighs. He finally pulled his mouth away. "God, Gillian, I've been wanting to do that for so long—"

"Not as long as I have." I traced the outline of his mouth with my finger.

"I have a confession to make. After that night with . . . you know who . . . I thought about you constantly. I've never been so preoccupied with a woman. I wanted to have sex with you again—and I wanted more than that. But I figured you probably weren't interested in seeing me again. After all, you were busy with . . . that other person. Then I heard he was engaged. I started taking walks past your building—every single day—

hoping I'd 'accidentally' run into you. Then one morning I saw you come out of your building with another guy. He was good-looking—short and blond."

"That must have been Justin."

"I guess so. You didn't see me; I was across the street. You and Justin were laughing. You seemed happy with him. So I gave up. I stopped wandering around your neighborhood and tried to forget about you completely. Then just a few weeks later, there you were, at the shoot for Hudson's."

I squirmed with happiness. "It must have been fate."

"I don't know what it was, but I was so glad to see you. I felt an even stronger connection to you. And I wanted you so much—it was difficult to control myself. I wanted to rip your clothes off and make love to you right there on the set."

"I wouldn't have objected. You could have ravished me right then and there. But what about Sophie?"

"My roommate, Carl, introduced us. He's dating Sophie's best friend. I liked Sophie, but as I said before, we just weren't right for each other."

I plucked at some grass blades. "It's my turn to confess. After we had sex that night, I thought about you, too. Constantly. I fantasized about you—not just sexually. I tried to make it work with Justin, but I just didn't want him the way I wanted you. I nearly passed out when I saw you on the set of the commercial. I was hoping you'd ask me out after the shoot.... When you didn't, I decided you'd been friendly just to be nice. Then I saw you at Joanne's party with Sophie, and I was devastated. I imagined that you considered me a slut... not someone you'd ever want to date seriously. And Sophie seemed so perfect...."

"She is perfect—for another man. Gillian, I never thought of you as a slut. That night with you was the most erotic experience I've ever had. It would have been even better if we'd been alone."

I laughed nervously. "It was wonderful for me, too, even though the situation was weird."

"Gillian. . . ." Greg pulled me into his arms. I rested my head against his chest and relished the sensation of his heartbeat and even breathing. We remained peacefully entwined for a long time. Finally Greg broke the silence. "I think this could be the start of something amazing, Gillian. I really want it to work out between us. We should take things slowly."

I pulled away from his embrace and looked into his eyes. "Because of what happened that first time we met?"

"Yes. I think we need to establish a strong friendship before we get sexually involved."

I rested my head against his chest again. "I know you're right . . . but, god, it's going to be hard to keep my hands off you."

Greg's laugh was strained. "It's hard for me, too . . . believe me."

I glanced down and noticed the huge bulge straining against his fly. "My goodness. How did that happen?" I gently pressed the palm of my hand against his crotch.

"God, Gillian. Please don't. I might explode."

I pulled my hand away—as slowly as possible. "I'm almost ready to explode, too. I don't know how long we can hold out, but perhaps the anticipation will make it even better when we finally go to bed."

"I'm sure it will. Gillian, it's going to be so good. All of it." His warm brown eyes met mine, and I knew I had fallen in love.

19

When I woke up the next morning, I stretched luxuriously and wondered why I felt so happy. An amazingly vivid dream slowly came back to me . . . something about a picnic with Greg. Then the wonderful reality hit me—it hadn't been a dream. It had actually happened. Greg had feelings for me. We were dating. And I was in love with him.

I sighed as I remembered his insistence on a purely platonic relationship. I knew he was right about taking things slowly, but I wanted him so much. . . . I decided I had to ignore Miss Hornypants for the next few weeks.

I called Anita to let her know I had news to share. She suggested meeting at a coffee shop on Broadway for breakfast. As we waited for our eggs benedict, I noticed that Anita was in a great mood—she seemed nearly as happy as I was. She said she'd gone out with Miles the night before—and had gone to bed with him. "It was fantastic, even better than I'd thought it would be," she gushed.

"Well, to quote your own words back at you, you have the radiant glow of a well-fucked woman," I said.

She grinned. "And that's the best kind of radiant glow. Now tell me your news."

"Okay. You remember Greg Warren? The actor who played my fiancé in the Hudson's commercial."

"Sure. Tall, dark guy with curly, dark hair. Very cute—and you were very attracted to him."

"We've been spending time together—just as friends. Yesterday we had a picnic lunch in Central Park. He told me he'd broken up with Sophie—the French girl—and had feelings for me."

Anita's eyes lit up. "That's terrific. Of course I've never met this guy, but he sounds more interesting than Justin—and he has to be nicer than David. So have you gone to bed with him yet?"

"Uh, no." I carefully stirred cream into my coffee, hoping Anita wouldn't pick up on my little white lie. "We decided to take things slowly. This past year has been a little rough for me emotionally, so we're going to wait a while before we take it to the next level."

Anita raised her eyebrows. "This guy must be exceptional. Most men want sex ASAP."

"Oh, Anita, he *is* exceptional. So smart and funny and sweet—and he's an incredible cook."

"Boy, you've fallen hard. I can identify. Miles seems to be the perfect man for me. He's going to San Francisco on business next week and wants me to come with him. Ordinarily I'd feel hesitant about traveling with a guy I've known for such a short time, but I feel like I've known Miles forever."

We spent the next half hour drinking coffee and raving about our new men. "It feels like a turning point for us," said Anita. "Maybe we've finally found the right guys."

"I think you're right," I replied. "I have a very good feeling about Greg and Miles."

* * *

Greg and I were both busy with auditions during the next few days. But we talked to each other every night, sometimes for over an hour. He gave me his cell-phone number; I had to resist the temptation to call him every five minutes. On the subway I even doodled his name on bits of scrap paper. I was completely regressing to a thirteen-year-old mindset—and I didn't care.

We made a date for pizza and a movie. We chatted and laughed over a pepperoni and onion pie, exchanging garlic-infused kisses between bites. The movie was a lame romantic comedy with very few laughs and a barely discernable plot, but we didn't mind. I snuggled into the crook of Greg's arm and felt like I'd achieved a state of nirvana.

We held hands as we strolled back to my apartment. As soon as I shut the front door behind us, Greg kissed me lightly on the forehead.

"Do you want some coffee?" I asked.

"No, I want you," he said, skimming a finger along my cheek and down my throat.

I swallowed hard. "Do you mean . . ."

"No. Not quite yet. But I want to kiss you and hold you."

We sat on the sofa, and I nestled into his embrace. I massaged his neck and shoulders, relishing the hardness of his smooth muscles under his T-shirt. He pulled me closer and kissed me softly. I took his hand and placed it on my right breast. My nipple immediately stiffened. Greg sighed, sliding his hand up my shirt and underneath my bra. "So soft," he murmured. His warm fingers felt wonderful on my skin. I kissed him with more urgency, my tongue probing deeply. I reached down and rubbed the enormous bulge of his hard cock.

We kissed for a long time. My pussy ached; the throbbing was almost unbearable. I remembered frustrating make-out sessions in high school—getting so excited and being too scared to "go all the way."

We finally came up for air. "Greg," I panted. "Are you sure you want to wait?"

"Yes. I really want to make love to you, Gillian . . . but I want the first time to be special." His voice sounded ready to break.

"It won't exactly be the first time. But I understand what you mean." I flopped back against the cushions, trying to suppress my disappointment.

Greg leaned forward and stroked my hair. "Gillian . . . how about this . . . let's spend a weekend together on the Cape. A friend of mine just opened a B and B in Falmouth—he'll give us a good rate. It will be fun and romantic."

I sat up, my frustration and disappointment quickly dissolving. "That sounds wonderful. Could we go this weekend? I don't think I can hold out much longer."

Greg smiled. "I'll give Ben a call tomorrow and ask him to hold his best room for us. I have a car—a beat-up Subaru, but it still runs. We could drive up Friday night."

I flung my arms around his neck. "That would be perfect. Oh, Greg, I can't wait. I just hope this B and B has thick walls. I think we're going to be a little noisy."

Greg finally left around midnight. As soon as he was gone, I leaned against the front door and pulled up my skirt. I yanked my panties down and rubbed my clit, thinking about his warm, wet tongue. I came within a minute. In bed, I still felt too excited—physically and mentally—to fall asleep. I wondered if Greg was also horny. I thought about him masturbating and felt the insistent warmth throbbing in my pussy again. I spread my legs and slid three fingers inside my pussy, imagining Greg's long, thick shaft. When I came again I finally felt relaxed enough to sleep.

Greg called me the next morning to say he'd booked a room

for us at Ben's B and B. "I'll pick you up on Friday. Is noon okay?"

"Yes. Oh, Greg, I'm looking forward to this so much."

"Me, too. I think it's going to be a memorable weekend."

"The best ever. I'm sure of it."

After we hung up, I called Anita to let her know about my trip to the Cape with Greg. "Are you finally going to make love?" she asked.

"Yes, yes, yes. I can't wait. I just hope it's as good as we remember it. I mean, as we think it will be." I bit my lip, hoping Anita hadn't noticed my slip-up.

She was too preoccupied to catch it. "Well, have a wonderful time—in bed and out of bed. Tomorrow I'm off to San Francisco with Miles. Can you believe this? Both of us are going on romantic trips with hot guys. Our karma must be really good right now."

We made a date to meet at Java Java when we were both back in town. After I hung up I pulled my suitcase out of the closet and wondered what to pack. I decided to splurge on new underwear. I wanted to look as sexy as possible for Greg.

I spent nearly a hundred dollars on push-up bras and matching panties, a bustier and a lacy garter belt with stockings. I felt well equipped enough to open a bordello. I also packed jeans, shorts, T-shirts, sweaters (in case it was chilly at night), a bikini with matching cover-up, a few sundresses, two nighties and a robe, sandals, sneakers and a pair of high-heeled pumps. Also belts, jewelry and other accessories. I had to struggle with the zipper for five minutes to get the suitcase closed.

When Greg picked me up the following day, his eyes widened at the sight of my bulging suitcase. "Jesus, Gillian, we're going for only two days. It looks like you packed enough for a month."

I gave an embarrassed laugh. "I know. I just want to be prepared."

"Cape Cod isn't exactly the wilderness." But he grinned as he heaved my bag into the trunk, and I knew he wasn't truly annoyed. His luggage consisted of a single backpack.

The drive to the Cape was long, but the time seemed to fly by. We occupied ourselves by singing silly songs. Greg's voice was nearly as bad as mine. In Connecticut we stopped for a late lunch at a café with a wonderful outdoor deck overlooking the Long Island Sound. As we sped through Rhode Island towards Massachusetts, Greg asked, "Have you ever been to the Cape?"

"Just once, with my family. My parents rented a cottage for a week when I was ten and my sister, Caroline, was four. It rained nearly the whole time. Then Caroline and I got into some poison ivy, and we were covered with itchy rashes. It wasn't a great experience."

Greg smiled and reached over to intertwine his fingers with mine. "Sorry to hear that. I'm sure this trip will be more enjoyable."

"Yes," I whispered, thinking about the coming night.

"We can visit my mom in Sandwich—it's not far. But if you don't want to, I'll understand."

"I'd love to meet your mom." Ordinarily I'd feel nervous about taking the big "meet the parents" step, but I felt completely at ease with Greg.

We arrived in Falmouth in the early evening, pulling up in front of an enormous white Victorian house. I was enchanted by the turrets, widow's walk and gingerbread trim. The swing seat and rocking chairs on the wraparound porch looked inviting. The surrounding gardens were bursting with lilies, hydrangeas and roses.

"Oh Greg, it's wonderful. I can't imagine a more romantic place."

"I thought you'd like it." He pulled me up the stairs and

through the front door. Ben greeted us in the foyer. He was a cheerful, short guy who reminded me of Sam the Hobbit.

"Ben, this place is so beautiful and charming—it looks like it belongs in a fairy tale," I said.

"Thanks. I wish I could take all the credit, but most of this is my grandmother's doing. She lived here for over forty years. She loved to garden—planted all those flowers and bushes. When she died last year she left the house to me and my brother, Tom. We talked about selling the place but just couldn't go through with it. So we ended up opening this B and B. Business has been good so far."

Ben lugged my bulging suitcase up the gracefully curving staircase. He opened the door to what must have once been the master bedroom. I gasped with delight. A border of white violets ran around the top of pale yellow walls. The enormous windows were framed by white lace curtains. A matching white lace coverlet was spread across the king-size cherry-wood bed. Bright throw rugs were scattered across the highly polished wide planks of the wood floor. The room was filled with a sweet fragrance emanating from jars of white and pink roses.

"Perfect," I whispered.

"Well, I'll let you two unpack and settle in," said Ben, tactfully withdrawing.

I threw my arms around Greg's neck. "Thank you so much. You were right. It was worth the wait. This is so special."

Greg squeezed me tight. I felt his heart pounding against mine. "I love to make you happy, Gillian." He pressed his lips against my throat. A deep shiver of anticipation ran through my body. I lifted my face to his, and he kissed me hard and deep. As his tongue played with mine, I felt a surge of desire that nearly overwhelmed me.

Greg released my mouth."Gillian . . . let's try out this bed." His voice was husky.

"I'd love to take it for a test drive." I laughed.

We slipped off our shoes and fell together on the bed. Greg gazed into my eyes as he slowly unbuttoned my blouse. He massaged my hard nipples through the sheer silk of my bra. My breathing became ragged. I impatiently yanked his T-shirt up over his head and threw it on the floor. I covered the smooth skin of his broad chest with kisses.

We both lost control. Greg fumbled with the hooks of my bra and finally released my breasts, kissing and licking and sucking my rosy nipples. The intensity of the pleasure made me whimper. He unzipped my shorts and tossed them on the growing pile of clothing on the floor. He rolled on top of me. I spread my legs so I could feel his enormous hard-on pressing against my pussy. He kissed me until my lips were swollen. I pressed his head against my breasts and inhaled his wonderful earthy smell.

"Tell me what you want, Gillian. I'll do anything to please you," he murmured.

"Tease me. . . . Leave my panties on and use your tongue and fingers to excite me."

He gently stroked my pussy through the fine black lace.

"Oh, god, that feels so good. . . ."

He knelt between my legs and flicked his tongue across my clit, lightly and slowly at first and then harder and faster. I grasped his head and cried out as an unexpected orgasm racked my body.

He stared at me as I lay there panting. "You're so beautiful, Gillian. I can't wait . . . I have to take you now."

He unzipped his fly and pulled out his long, thick shaft. I stared at the droplets of cum beading on the head. He pulled my panties to one side and plunged deep into me. As he slowly pumped in and out, the fine lace rubbed against my clit and lips. I wrapped my legs around his waist and put my hands on his ass, pulling him deeper into me.

"Gillian. . . ." he said through gritted teeth. Sweat broke out on his forehead. I knew he was struggling to hold back, trying not to come until he'd given me another orgasm.

I closed my eyes and abandoned myself to sensation. Nothing in the world existed except Greg and the exquisite pleasure. I felt the slow spiral of pleasure accelerate and intensify. I screamed as I came hard, digging my nails into Greg's ass.

He pumped faster and finally let out a long groan as he exploded inside me. He collapsed on my chest. I stroked his sweat-soaked hair and shoulders as our breathing slowed.

He raised his head to look at me. "Well? Did my performance meet your expectations?"

"Oh, yes," I whispered. "You passed the audition with flying colors. But I'll need you for a callback. In fact, several call backs. Daily and nightly callbacks."

We both burst into laughter.

We took a bath together in the huge claw-foot tub. Ben had provided lilac bubble bath. "I hope it's not too girlie for you," I said.

"Well, I'd prefer beer-scented bubble bath, but this is okay. My masculinity isn't too threatened." Greg leaned back. I felt his foot massaging my thigh.

I gave a long sigh of contentment. "I don't think I've ever been so happy. It's so hard to believe we're here together, after all we've been through."

Greg leaned forward to kiss my nose. "I know. And this is just the beginning. We have so much to look forward to. . . ." He kissed my nose again and then drifted lower to kiss my mouth. I closed my eyes and parted my lips to welcome his tongue. I reached down and found his hard-on beneath the bubbles. I slid it into my pussy and rocked gently as he moaned. He ran his hands over my soapy breasts.

"Stay still," I murmured. "Perfectly still. Let me hump your cock. . . ." I rocked faster, gripping his shoulders and squeezing my pussy around his shaft. I stopped for a moment, making him groan. Then I started again, rocking harder, whispering his name over and over. We came simultaneously, our cries mingling and echoing.

We made love again in the big four-poster bed before falling into an exhausted sleep. I was awakened the next morning by a strange, delightful sensation. I sleepily stretched and opened my eyes. I saw Greg's face between my thighs; he was licking my pussy. I undulated beneath his warm, wet tongue. I thought my clit would burst. "Oh, god . . ." I gasped. I came within moments.

Greg waited a moment for me to recover. He started to slide his shaft into me, but I stopped him. "I'm a little sore from last night," I whispered.

"Oh, sorry."

I smiled. "Don't apologize. I have other ideas for satisfying you. Straddle my face. I want to suck your cock until you scream."

He seemed very enthusiastic about that idea. He kneeled so his cock was directly over my mouth. I held the shaft and licked the head vigorously and then ran my tongue up and down the length and all over his balls. "Gillian . . ." he moaned, "that feels so good . . . don't stop. . . ."

I licked and sucked for a long time; whenever he seemed on the brink of spurting, I'd stop until he begged me to start again. Finally I opened my mouth for him. He slowly slid his long shaft all the way in and then slid it all the way out. He repeated the motion, increasing the tempo. I gently squeezed his balls. He pumped very fast until I felt a deep convulsion at the base of his shaft. He groaned and shuddered as he shot his cum into my mouth. I swallowed the warm, salty-sweet liquid.

He pulled his cock out of my mouth and collapsed against

the pillows. He wrapped his arms around me and interwined his legs with mine. "Thanks, darling, that was incredible." He sighed.

"The pleasure was all mine," I purred. "Sex with you is so amazing. It's tender but raunchy at the same time. Sweet and filthy—just the way I like it."

Greg grinned. "That's how I like it, too. I think we're going to have a lot of fun exploring . . . discovering the best ways to please each other."

We finally managed to drag ourselves out of bed and got dressed. We were ravenous—we'd skipped dinner the night before. Ben served us incredible blueberry pancakes and spicy sausage. We sat on the front porch and wolfed down our breakfast.

It was a spectacular summer day. We strolled the Shining Sea Bikeway from Falmouth all the way to Woods Hole. The view of the ocean with the hump of Martha's Vineyard on the horizon was breathtaking. The salty breeze, fragrant beach roses and the warm security of my hand in Greg's surrounded me with bliss. We ate scrumptious clam chowder and salad at a cozy restaurant in Woods Hole.

As we walked slowly back to Falmouth on the bike path, Greg pointed out the ferry chugging from Woods Hole to Martha's Vineyard. "The next time we come up here, we'll have to spend a day on the Vineyard."

"I'd love that. I've never been there. . . . I've heard wonderful things about the Vineyard." The thought of a future trip with Greg made me radiate with joy.

Back at the B and B Greg called his mother. She invited us for dinner, and Greg accepted. I felt a twinge of nervousness as we drove to her house. Things were going so well with Greg—almost too well. What if his mother turned out to be a witch, determined to poison our happiness?

I should have known better. Any woman who had produced

a son like Greg had to be delightful. She greeted us at the door of her rambling farmhouse and immediately gave me a hug. "So you're Gillian. Greg has told me so much about you. He said you were extremely pretty, and he certainly didn't exaggerate."

I blushed. "Thank you, Mrs. Warren."

"Please, you must call me Celeste. When people call me Mrs. Warren I feel about ninety years old."

Celeste was a petite woman with Greg's curly dark hair and deep brown eyes. She had a well-preserved, mature beauty. I wondered why she had never remarried; any man with an ounce of taste would have found her attractive. Perhaps she had loved Greg's father too much. . . . I glanced at Greg, and my heart contracted at the thought of losing him.

I was distracted from this morbid thought by the arrival of Ryan, Greg's younger brother. Ryan was a pale copy of Greg—he was shorter and thinner and not quite as handsome. But he was every bit as charming.

We sat on the patio drinking white wine as Ryan grilled swordfish. We talked easily about the Cape, New Hampshire and New York. I nearly choked on my wine when Ryan asked how Greg and I had met. Greg wasn't fazed at all. "We met on the set of the commercial for Hudson's," he said casually.

As we ate dinner on the patio, Celeste explained that she still worked as an elementary school teacher but was on the verge of retirement. Ryan was following in her footsteps; he was close to obtaining his certification. "I'm the only bohemian in the family," Greg joked.

I looked around the expansive yard—a tire swing hung from an enormous oak tree, and a brook babbled near an ancient stone wall. "It must have been wonderful to grow up here. This fantastic house and huge yard . . . the ocean and the beaches so close by . . ."

"It was great," said Ryan. "We were lucky kids." There was

a moment of prolonged silence. I suddenly remembered the terrible loss that had nearly shattered their lives—the sudden death of Mr. Warren. I bit my lip.

Greg glanced at me and seemed to understand. "I don't know about the rest of you, but I could use some exercise after that huge dinner. Let's clean up and then go for a walk on the boardwalk."

The mood shifted. We joked and laughed as we carried dishes into the kitchen. Celeste's golden retriever helped by thoroughly licking the plates before we loaded them in the dishwasher.

The Sandwich boardwalk stretched across a marsh to a beach. Greg pointed out a huge osprey nest perched on a pole in the marsh grass. An osprey with a fish in his mouth flew to the nest, and we watched his mate feed the screaming fledglings.

We walked to the beach and sat on the boulders of a breakwater. Sailboats and small motor boats glided toward the entrance of the Cape Cod Canal. As evening fell, ribbons of pink and lavender streaked the sky. A silvery crescent moon was revealed as the horizon deepened from blue to gray. Greg wrapped his arm around me and kissed my cheek. "You two look so sweet together," Celeste murmured.

"Geez, Mom, don't embarrass me," groaned Greg with a roll of his eyes.

"I can't resist. It's been so easy . . . ever since you were twelve and started chasing girls."

I smiled and squeezed Greg's hand. "So you were a juvenile Don Juan. I wish I'd known you back then. I would have had such a crush on you. . . ."

We finally left when the air turned chilly and the mosquitoes came out in force. We said our good-byes on the front steps of Celeste's house. "Please come back soon," she said, giving me another hug. I knew she was sincere. Celeste was a no-bullshit kind of person—just like her sons.

* * *

Back at the B and B, we made love slowly and sleepily. Greg covered every inch of my body with soft kisses. He gently pulled my legs apart and kissed my mound. His tongue teased my clit until I was writhing and panting. I took his shaft in my hand and pressed the head of his cock against my clit. He slid into me slowly, starting a languorous rhythm. I stared into his eyes, loving the hot desire I saw there. He pumped harder until I was begging for release. I finally came, clenching my thighs tightly around his back as he exploded in me. When we were sated, I fell asleep in the shelter of Greg's embrace.

The following morning it was cool and cloudy; a fine, misty rain fell. After breakfast we went for a short walk and bought the Sunday papers. We spent most of the day in bed, naked, alternately reading and making love. I smiled when I thought about the huge wardrobe I'd packed. I hadn't even had a chance to wear the sexy lingerie—at least not for very long. Greg was so hot for me he simply tore it off.

During one of our newspaper breaks I browsed a gossip column. "Greg? Do you think Angelina Jolie is attractive?"

He glanced up from the sports section. "Not really. Her lips scare me."

"What about Pamela Anderson?"

"No. Her boobs scare me. Every time I see a picture of her I immediately think of bowling balls."

"Paris Hilton?"

"God, she *really* scares me. She looks like an alien from the planet Tanorexia."

I swatted him with the paper and burst out laughing. "You're just trying to pacify me."

"Not true. You're my type, Gillian. I have a thing for sexy little brunettes with blue eyes. . . ." He shoved the newspapers to the floor and leaned forward to untie the belt of my silk robe.

"Tell me what you like about my body."

"I love your sweet little ass." He cupped my cheeks. "And your sweet round breasts." He kissed each nipple. "And your sweet tight pussy." He slowly spread my legs. "It's always so wet and warm. And you have such a big pink clit."

"A big pink clit and a dirty little mind." I laughed.

"Yes, I love your dirty little mind best of all."

I sank against the pillows and closed my eyes, ready for another long, slow journey to a shattering climax.

We left for New York early the next morning. I felt wistful. It was difficult to leave—we'd had such a wonderful time—but Greg promised Ben we'd return soon. We spent most of the long drive home in companionable silence, reveling in each other's presence—and dreaming of a blissful future together.

20

I couldn't wait to tell Anita all about my glorious weekend. I called her cell to confirm our meeting at Java Java. I got her voice mail and left a message. I was surprised when she didn't call me back; it was unlike her. I decided to just show up at Java Java. I assumed she'd be there.

I arrived at the café and glanced around. No sign of her. I took a seat at our usual table, ordered a scone and a latte and watched the door for Anita. After ten minutes had gone by I became worried. I called her cell and reached her voice mail again. I left another message, wondering where on earth she could be.

As soon as I flipped my phone closed I saw Anita in the doorway. I called to her, feeling a rush of relief. She sat down opposite me and pulled her sunglasses from her face. Her eyes were red and swollen.

"Anita! What happened?"

Anita turned away to give her order to the hovering waitress. When she turned back to me, I could see she was on the verge of crying.

"That bastard Miles," she hissed. "He's married."

I was stunned. "Oh, my god. How did you find out?"

"We were staying at this spectacular hotel in San Francisco. Miles booked the most extravagant suite. We were having so much fun—and having great sex. Then one afternoon he was in the shower. His cell phone rang, and he yelled from the shower that he was expecting an important call from a business associate. He asked me to answer it. It was his wife, calling from London."

"Oh, Christ, Anita," I whispered.

She rubbed her bloodshot eyes. "The wife—her name is Jessica—didn't seem fazed. When I confronted Miles he said they have an arrangement. Apparently Jessica doesn't give a shit if he sleeps with other women when he's away on business. Miles couldn't understand why I was so upset. He seemed to think it was obvious that we were just having a fling."

"What a jerk! I hope you ripped him a new one."

Anita laughed bitterly. "Oh, I wanted to, believe me. I settled for throwing a few expensive objets d'art at him. I missed him—but the hotel management is going to hand him a very hefty bill for the damage."

"Good! Maybe he'll be banned from all the hotels in the chain."

"Yes, that would be great. . . ." Anita said faintly. Again she looked ready to burst into tears. "Gillian, this hurts so much. I really thought he might be the love of my life. . . ."

"Let's get out of here," I said, tossing a $10 bill on the table. "Come back to my place. We'll spend the day together, and we'll get your mind and heart back in shape."

Anita and I talked, baked and ate chocolate chip cookies, watched a few soap operas. At times she seemed to be recovering from the shock. But after cracking a joke or making a nasty remark about Miles, her eyes would fill with tears again.

I had planned to spend the evening—and the night—with Greg, but I knew Anita was too fragile. I invited her to spend the night at my place; she gratefully accepted. I called Greg and explained the situation to him. "I'm so sorry about this. I know you really wanted to see me tonight," I said apologetically.

"Hey, it's okay. I miss you so much already, but I understand completely. Let's get together tomorrow night."

"You are the sweetest, kindest, most wonderful man in the world."

"Didn't you know? I was Gandhi in my last life," he joked.

After I hung up, Anita sighed. "At least one of us found a terrific guy. Now tell me everything about your weekend on the Cape."

It seemed almost cruel to gush about my happiness, but Anita was genuinely glad for me. I described nearly every moment of our trip in minute detail. She listened intently and seemed distracted from her misery—for the moment.

We went to bed early. I heard Anita sniffling in the darkness. I stroked her hair until she fell asleep.

I spent a lot of time with Anita over the next few weeks, trying to help her get past the shock and pain. I remembered how much she'd helped me after the fiasco with David. In the past Anita had cured a broken heart by finding another man immediately. This time was different. I was glad she wasn't eager to rush headlong into another affair.

I spent the rest of my free time with Greg. Every moment with him filled me with joy. Even the most mundane chores—grocery shopping, doing laundry, cooking—were fun with Greg. It all seemed so perfect that I kept expecting some disaster to strike—but our relationship grew stronger daily.

He showed me the apartment on West Eighty-Fifth Street that he shared with his friend Carl. It was a bit small, but I was relieved to discover that it didn't smell like sour milk or old pizza like Justin's studio. The furnishings were a little more sophisticated than the usual bachelor-pad decor. Greg and Carl had graduated from college-dorm milk crates and futons to Ikea chairs and tables.

I liked Carl, his easygoing roommate, but I felt more comfortable at my apartment. We had more room and more privacy there—very necessary for our wild lovemaking. Greg spent nearly every night with me. I gave him keys to the building and apartment. I was tempted to ask him to move in with me, but I didn't want to make him nervous or jeopardize our romance. I also had to resist the temptation to blurt out, "I love you." I kept hoping to hear those words from him first.

We decided to throw a party at my place, a sort of "coming out as a couple" event for our friends. We invited quite a crowd, including Carl, Anita, Steve and Oliver, Natalie, and Chris and Nancy. When I called Joanne to invite her and Heather, she said, "Aha! I knew it! You and Greg weren't acting during the last take of that Hudson's shoot. It was so obvious that something was going on. And at my party he couldn't keep his eyes off you. I'm glad you two finally got together."

"Thanks. It wasn't easy—I thought it was never going to happen. But it finally did, and we're incredibly happy."

When I called Aunt Mary, I didn't expect her to accept the invitation, but it turned out she was coming to Manhattan that weekend anyway. She said she'd love to come to the party. "I look forward to meeting Greg. I liked Justin a lot, but it sounds like this man is your soul mate," she said.

"Oh, yes," I replied with a sigh of bliss. "I'm so glad you're coming. It seems like ages since we last saw each other."

Every person we invited accepted the invitation. On the day of the party I cleaned frantically while Greg cooked. He produced the most amazing hors d'oeuvres—lobster dip, hot artichoke tarts, a spicy nut mix.

The party was a smashing success. Everyone had a great time. The only minor problem was Natalie—I had to prevent her from trying to set Anita up with Carl and every other single man in the room.

Not surprisingly, all my friends loved Greg. "That Justin was nice," said Mary, "but Greg . . . he's exceptional."

"I know. I feel so lucky." I glanced across the room and met Greg's eyes. He smiled, and I felt a surge of desire. I wanted everyone to leave so I could ravish him.

The last guest departed well after midnight. Greg shut the front door and then immediately turned to me and crushed me in his arms. "You looked so gorgeous tonight," he whispered in my ear. "I've been lusting for you for hours."

"I know . . . I want you, too. So much . . ."

We kissed long and hard, our hands exploring sensitive places. My pussy ached; I grasped Greg's hips and ground my crotch against his hard-on. "I need your cock right now," I panted. I sat on the sofa and pulled up my skirt. Greg kneeled between my open legs and unzipped his fly.

"Right now, fuck me now," I demanded. He pulled my panties aside and slid his cock all the way into my wet pussy. He remained still; I moaned with frustration.

"Easy, Gillian," he murmured. He gently rubbed the pink nub of my clit with his thumb.

I squirmed. "Give it to me, Greg. Please give me your cock. Make me come, make me scream—"

He suddenly thrust hard. "Do you like that?"

"Yes, yes, keep fucking me—"

He thrust hard again and again until the pulsating sensation in my pussy became unbearable. I cried out in ecstasy. A moment later he groaned with his final thrust. I felt the warm gush of cum filling my pussy.

I sighed. "That was . . . delicious."

"My hors d'oeuvres or my lovemaking?" Greg teased.

"Both. You're a man of many talents." I rested my head against his chest, feeling utterly content.

Our professional lives were nearly as satisfying as our personal lives. Oliver called to let me know a new character was being introduced on *Nights of Passion*—Serena, a ruthless nympho who would do anything to get what she wanted.

"It sounds like a wonderfully juicy part—lots of opportunities to camp it up," I said.

"I'm sure your agent can arrange an audition," said Oliver. "And I'll put in a good word for you with the casting director and the producers."

I'd never played a character like Serena before, but the audition went well—I knew I'd impressed everyone. I wasn't surprised when the casting director requested a callback—but I was still very excited. Serena was a major new character, scheduled to appear in at least twenty-six episodes. The idea of a steady gig was heavenly.

When Ellen called me to let me know I had the part, I nearly cried with happiness. That night I took Greg out to celebrate. I treated him to dinner at Tuscan Sun, a wildly expensive new Italian restaurant. The extravagant meal was worth every penny.

"This veal marsala is even better than my cousin Marc's—and I didn't think that was possible," said Greg. He looked so handsome in his pearl-gray suit and blue silk tie. I'd never seen him dressed formally.

I leaned across the table to give him a kiss. "You clean up very nicely. I'm so proud to be with you. Every woman in the room is staring at you . . . and feeling jealous of me."

Greg laughed. "I think you've already slipped into Serena's persona—you'll resort to any kind of flattery to get what you want."

"And what do you think I want?'

"Let me guess . . . you want to seduce me and use my body for your own pleasure."

"Bingo! I want you to be my stud."

"Sounds like a challenge, but I'll do my best."

That night Greg surprised me in bed. We tried positions I hadn't even known existed. As I lay on my back he knelt between my legs and hooked his arms under my knees, lifting my hips high. He plunged deep into me. "Play with your pussy, Gillian," he said.

I rubbed my pussy lips together as he slowly pumped in and out. "Harder . . . faster," I ordered. He thrust into me with more power. "That's it . . ." I whispered, "make me come. . . ." I used my index finger to rub my engorged clit. I screamed Greg's name as an orgasm burst through me.

Greg was able to hold back. He pulled his rigid cock out of my pussy. I pushed him onto his back and squeezed my breasts around his shaft. I spread his legs and licked his balls, slowly working my way up the length of his cock to the head. Finally I straddled his hips and rubbed the head of his cock against my pussy lips. With one hand I spread my lips and massaged my clit with his cock. "God, Gillian, that feels incredible," he whispered.

"Do you want me to sit on your cock?"

"Yes, I want you to ride me. . . ."

I slowly slid his shaft into my pussy. I squeezed my muscles around his cock. He reached up to play with my hard nipples. I rocked in a gentle rhythm, slowly increasing the tempo. Greg's eyes were half closed, his mouth parted slightly. I grasped the base of his cock and pumped my pussy up and down the length of his shaft. I felt another orgasm building; Greg opened his eyes and stared at me as I came again, even harder this time.

He still didn't come. "My god, did you take some kind of pill?" I asked in amazement.

"No . . . I'm just holding back until you're completely satisfied. I take my studly duties very seriously," he said with a grin.

He pulled me to the edge of the bed and turned me over on my side. He separated my legs so I was in a scissors position, my vagina exposed. He stood by the side of the bed and thrust his cock into me hard. I gasped at the sensation—it was completely different from anything I'd felt before.

Once again I played with my clit and lips while he fucked me. The orgasm was slow to build; when I finally came the pleasure nearly overwhelmed me. I heard Greg's long, deep groan as he spurted.

We lay on the bed together, completely spent. "My god," I murmured.

"'My god' is right." Greg rolled over and nuzzled my breasts. "I hope sex will never be boring for us."

"I don't think that's possible; the word *boring* doesn't exist in your vocabulary," I replied with a contented yawn. Within minutes we were asleep, exhausted and sated.

A few weeks later Greg's lucky break came through. He tried out for the lead role in a new TV series about a pro baseball player who decides to become a PI after an injury ruins his career. The casting director requested two callbacks after the initial audition. Greg wanted the role of Matt Blake as badly as I had wanted the role of Serena. "I've seen only one script, but the writing is exceptional," he said. "And the network is willing to invest a lot in this series. If the ratings are decent, it could run for a long time."

"Wouldn't that be incredible—both of us with starring roles in long-running shows?" I said exultantly. "I'm afraid to even hope you'll get the role. I don't want to jinx it."

I spent a day shopping with Anita. When I came home that evening, I found my apartment filled with fresh flowers and candles. The delicious smell of chicken cordon bleu wafted from the kitchen. Greg emerged with a bottle of champagne and two new champagne flutes.

"You got the part!" I threw my arms around his neck, throwing him off balance and nearly sending the bottle and glasses crashing to the floor.

"Yes, I got it." He put the bottle and glasses down on the coffee table and kissed me hard.

"I'm so happy and excited, I think I might burst."

We sat on the sofa, and Greg poured the champagne. I lifted my flute. "To ruthless nymphos and disabled athletes." Greg smiled at my toast, but I noticed he didn't seem nearly as ecstatic as I was.

I put down my champagne. "There's something wrong," I said flatly.

Greg looked me straight in the eyes. "Yes. The network execs have decided the series should be shot in LA. They want Chelsea Miller to play Matt's girlfriend, and Chelsea is insisting on staying in LA. She's not as big as she used to be, but she still has enough clout to make these demands."

"Oh, Christ." I closed my eyes and sank against the cushions. "So you'll have to move to LA."

Greg took my hand and squeezed it. "I know it's upsetting . . . believe me, I'm not happy about it either. But the network is green-lighting only one season at this point. So I might be out there for less than a year. We could manage the long-distance thing for that long. And if my series is picked up, you could move out to LA—"

"I don't know." I rubbed my face. "If things were different, I'd drop everything and move with you to LA in a heartbeat. But I've already signed the contract for *Nights of Passion.* And when we start working, we'll both have grueling schedules. We won't have much time to fly back and forth between New York and LA."

Greg was silent for a moment. "I know it's difficult, but I'm sure we can make it work. Gillian, you're the most important person in my life. I don't want our relationship to end just because we've both found success at the same time."

I leaned against his chest, and he stroked my hair. My eyes filled with tears. "I know you're sincere . . . and you're so important to me, too," I said in a choked voice. "I'm just so worried that our relationship won't survive a long separation."

Greg kissed my head. "All right, then. I won't take the part. You mean much more to me than a role in a TV series that might be off the air within a month."

"No!" I sat up straight. "You *have* to take the part, Greg. A chance like this is rare. You might not get another break. Go to LA—we'll make it work somehow."

"Are you sure about this?"

"Absolutely. I'd never forgive myself if some other actor became a big star because you passed on the series."

"Then I'll do it. Gillian . . . thank you so much for understanding."

During the rest of evening I tried hard to hide my distress. My appetite had vanished, but I pretended to enjoy Greg's chicken cordon bleu, grilled asparagus and chocolate mousse. After dinner we made love slowly and gently. This time I took charge. I rubbed warm massage oil into the firm muscles of his back, his legs and his ass. When he turned over, his cock was standing at attention. I pretended to ignore his enormous hard-on. I massaged his arms, his chest, his thighs and feet. A fine sheen of perspiration appeared on his face. I rubbed oil into his ab muscles and then trailed my fingers down to his cock. He stared as I flicked my tongue over his balls and head and then slid the entire length of his shaft into my mouth After sucking his cock for a long time, I straddled his face and spread my pussy lips. He licked eagerly, making me moan. I slid my wet pussy onto his hard shaft and rocked gently. He cupped my ass in his hands and thrust upward, deep into me. We came at exactly the same moment, both consumed by long, shuddering orgasms.

Greg immediately fell into a deep, satisfied sleep. I lay awake, anxious thoughts running through my mind. *How often will I be able to fly out to LA? How will I afford it? Chelsea Miller is such a party girl . . . and she has a slutty reputation. She doesn't have any qualms about going after men with wives or girlfriends. Greg will be working with her twelve hours a day . . . and some of his scenes with her will be romantic or sexy or both. . . .*

I fretted for hours. The pink light of dawn seeped slowly through the curtains. I closed my eyes and finally fell into a fitful, miserable slumber.

21

The next few days were the hardest of my life. I was so upset, anxious and depressed—and I couldn't let it show. I'd told Greg to take the part and go to LA. I knew if I revealed my misgivings, he'd change his mind—and I couldn't live with the guilt.

Of course I confided in Anita, and, as always, she did a great job of bolstering my spirits. "Okay, the next few months might be a little rough for you and Greg. But he really cares about you, he's not going to let this relationship go down the tubes."

"I hope you're right. But he's never said he loves me. I love him more than I've loved anyone, but I'm still not sure about the depth of his feelings. . . ."

"He loves you, Gillian. I'm sure of it. I've seen the way he looks at you. That's not just mild affection in his eyes."

"I know, I know. I'm just so scared, Anita. Losing Greg would be unbearable."

Anita kept offering positive reinforcement. "Look, I have an idea. I bought two tickets to a fashion charity ball—it's a fund-raiser for AIDS. But I'm not going to be able to go, that last-minute assignment in Milan came up. So why don't you go with Greg? It'll be a fun, romantic evening. It won't solve your problem, but perhaps it will make you feel even closer to Greg."

I gratefully accepted. "We've never been to an event like that—I'm sure Greg will enjoy it. Now for the important question: what shall I wear? I can't afford anything really extravagant."

Anita suggested we check out vintage-clothing boutiques. "I'll bet be can find something really pretty and unique for a couple hundred dollars."

We made a date to go shopping. I called Greg to tell him about the ball. "Sounds great," he said. "I bought a tuxedo a couple of years ago for a friend's formal wedding. I haven't had a chance to wear it since then. I hope it still fits."

"God, just the thought of you in a tuxedo makes me swoon," I joked. "I'm looking forward to this, Greg."

"Me, too. Gillian, thank you for being so supportive. I know you're not happy about my move to LA. I want to give you a special night."

I felt tears stinging my eyes again. "That's so sweet, Greg. It means a lot to me." I hung up before the tears overwhelmed me again.

Planning for the ball helped distract me from my misery. Anita and I hunted for days before we found the perfect dress. It was a 1950s strapless, pale blue, silk gown with a full skirt. "It's not Dior, but the designer was definitely influenced by his 'New Look' dresses," said Anita critically. "It's in excellent condition. It needs to be shortened an inch and taken in a bit at the bustline . . . but it's perfect for you. You look stunning."

As I twirled in front of the dressing-room mirror, I had to agree. The boutique owner showed us silver sandals and a small silver clutch bag. "I always thought these would be the perfect accessories for that dress," she said persuasively. Of course I had to have them. My tab came to over $600, which made me cringe.

Anita dismissed my worries with a wave of her hand. "You got a bargain. Besides, you and Greg are going to be stars—you both need to start dressing the part."

After the dress had been altered I modeled it for Greg. "What do you think?" I asked, pivoting slowly so he could get the full affect.

"Wow. I mean, *wow.* You always look great, but in that dress you look like an aristocrat. I'm going to look like a geek next to you."

I laughed. "It would be impossible for you to look geeky. I haven't decided what to do with my hair. I thought maybe I'd just wear it up in a simple French twist." I lifted my hair and coiled it. "How does this look?"

"Perfect. Your beautiful neck and shoulders are exposed . . . but you need some jewelry."

"I know. I haven't decided what to do about that. I'll ask Anita if she can lend me a couple of her good pieces."

"I'm sure she'll lend you something nice." Greg's fingers traced the line of my throat and shoulders down to my breasts. "Wonderful cleavage. . . ." He slipped his fingers under the bodice. "And hard nipples. . . ." He reached for the buttons, and the dress slid to the floor in a whisper of silk. I was standing nude except for the silver high-heeled sandals.

I wrapped my arms around Greg's waist and pressed my naked body against him. His fingers trailed down to my pussy and played with my triangle of hair. His touch was soft and delicate. I rubbed his hard-on through his jeans and blew my hot breath into his ear. I could feel his heart pounding through his thin cotton T-shirt. He gently parted my pussy lips and stroked my clit with one finger. I took his free hand and pushed three fingers inside my warm, wet opening. I pumped his fingers in and out as he gradually increased the pressure on my clit. The pleasure built to a crescendo. I convulsed around his fingers as waves of pleasure washed over me. Greg slid his fingers out of my pussy. I raised his hand to my mouth and licked off my juice.

"You're so sexy, Gillian . . . always full of surprises," Greg murmured.

"I have another surprise for you," I whispered. "Let's go to the bed."

In the bedroom he stood perfectly still while I stripped him. I dropped to my knees and licked and sucked his cock until he begged me to stop.

I lay on the bed and played with my pussy while he watched me and stroked his hard shaft. I took the hairbrush from my bedside table. I spread my lips and rubbed the handle against my clit. "I always come very hard when I do this," I said. "It works best when I'm on my knees. I want you enter me from behind and stay still until I tell you to move."

"Yes, I'd love that," he whispered.

I moved to the edge of the bed and turned over. I rested on my knees and forearms. Greg stood behind me and slid his cock deep into my pussy. He massaged my ass while I gently rubbed the brush handle against my clit. "Now," I said. "Fuck me slowly . . . and then harder and faster."

Greg pumped his shaft as I stroked my clit harder. The intensity of the pleasure was nearly unbearable. I screamed and bucked as I came. Greg suddenly pulled his cock from my pussy and shot his cum in the crevice of my ass. I loved the sensation of the warm, sticky fluid trickling down between my cheeks.

I collapsed on my stomach, panting hard, unable to move. Greg flopped down next to me. I was finally able to speak. "You're full of surprises, too. One of these days you're going to kill me with pleasure. But I can think of worse ways to go."

Greg smiled. "I think we'll probably go together." He cupped my face and stared into my eyes.

Say it, please say it, I thought desperately. *Say you love me.* But the words never came.

I was filled with anticipation as the night of the charity ball drew nearer. I was still unhappy about the situation with Greg; I needed a night of pure fun and extravagance.

Two days before the event, Greg called me. "Some bad news, Gillian. Well, not that bad. It's just a little inconvenient."

He sounded too casual. A feeling of dread knotted in my stomach. "What is it?"

"The director for the pilot and one of the producers will be in New York on Friday. They want to have dinner with me."

"But that's the night of the ball—"

"I know. But it doesn't start till eight. I asked Bill and Charlie to make an early reservation. I'm meeting them at six. I thought I'd drop my tuxedo off at your place tomorrow. I'll have an early dinner with these guys, swing by your place and change and then we can go to the ball. We might be a little late, but I'm sure we won't miss much."

"Oh . . . okay. I guess that will work," I said faintly.

"Great. I'll stop by tomorrow afternoon with my tux."

We hung up. I tried to figure out why I felt so disappointed—and a little angry. *That goddamned TV show is already causing problems for us. . . .*

"Don't be unreasonable," said Miss Prudence. *"Acting like a spoiled, clingy brat will drive Greg away. It's great that he has this meeting—another step forward in his career. You're still going to the ball, and you'll have a great time."*

I chewed my lower lip. I decided that I would ignore any negative thoughts about Greg's TV series. From now on I'd be Little Miss Supportive, helping Greg with his career any way I could.

* * *

Greg showed up the following afternoon with his tux and a square red velvet box tied with gold ribbons. "This is a little gift for Cinderella. To wear to the ball," he said.

I slowly pulled the ribbons away and lifted the top. I gasped with surprise. It was a set of pearls—three-strand choker, drop earrings and bracelet. "Oh, Greg, this is wonderful . . . but it's too much, too expensive. . . ."

"Don't worry about the expense. Remember, I'm a big star now," he said with a grin. I lifted my hair, and he hooked the choker around my throat. "Perfect," said Greg. I put on the earrings and bracelet. "Even more perfect," he said, kissing my nose.

The tears that came so easily these days filled my eyes again. "Thank you so much. This is the nicest present I've ever received. I mean it." I wrapped my arms around him and held him close. I came dangerously close to saying "I love you"—but I bit back the words.

I woke up on the day of the ball with a sense of delicious anticipation. I remained in bed for a few minutes, stretching slowly and thinking about the coming night. I was sure it would be special, the most romantic evening of my life. Perhaps Greg would finally say those three little words. . . .

I started to get ready hours in advance. I took a long bubble bath and then washed my hair under the shower, rinsing it with a chamomile infusion to bring out blond highlights. I painted my fingernails and toenails with a pale pink polish. I used a cucumber facial mask and shimmering body lotion to make my skin glow.

I wished I had Anita there to help me with my hair and makeup, but she'd left for Milan the day before. I tried to remember all the tricks she'd taught me as I applied makeup and twisted my hair into a chignon.

I finally slipped on the dress and silver high heels. I put on the pearl choker, bracelet and earrings. I dabbed Chanel No. 5 on my wrists and throat. I stared into a full-length mirror and almost didn't recognize myself. *I'll probably never look this pretty again,* I thought.

I sat down carefully on the sofa. I glanced at the clock. Seven thirty. Greg would be here soon. I picked up a magazine.

Twenty minutes later I put down the magazine and frowned at the clock. *Where is Greg? He should be here by now.* I thought about calling his cell, but I didn't want to interrupt his meeting. I tried to reassure myself: *He's probably on his way here.*

I turned on the TV and flipped through the channels, unable to focus on any of the programs. I finally allowed myself to look at the clock again. Eight twenty. Anxiety fluttered in my stomach. Perhaps Greg had been in an accident or had been mugged. . . .

I jumped at least a foot when my cell rang. "Hello?" I answered breathlessly.

"Hi, Gillian." *Greg.* Relief rushed through me. "We're just wrapping up here. I should be at your place in about forty-five minutes."

My relief dissolved under a wave of fury. "You're just wrapping up? You won't be here for another forty-five minutes?" I shrieked.

"Calm down, Gillian. I'm sorry about this—Bill and Charlie got caught in traffic, so they arrived at the restaurant late. And we had a lot to discuss—"

"I cannot believe this! You know how important this ball is to me—"

"Gillian, cut it out," Greg said sharply. "I said I was sorry. I can't fix it now. I'll be there as soon as I can."

I was trembling with rage. "I'm leaving. I'm going to the ball. I'll leave your ticket here in case you decide you want my company after all." I flipped my phone closed.

* * *

The charity ball was being held at a very elegant midtown hotel. During the cab ride I seethed with anger and hurt. I couldn't believe Greg had treated me in such a cavalier fashion. This was supposed to be the most romantic night of our lives, and he had ruined it. . . .

A tiny voice pointed out that I was overreacting and behaving childishly. I stubbornly ignored it. I choked back tears. I didn't want to wreck my makeup and show up at the ball looking like a mess.

By the time the cab stopped in front of the hotel's grand entrance, I had regained my composure. I sailed through the lobby with a serene smile on my face.

The ballroom was enormous, lit by huge, glittering chandeliers. An orchestra played Viennese waltzes. The crowd was chic, dressed to the nines in tuxedos and jewel-bright ball gowns. I sipped a glass of champagne and watched the dancers whirl by. I soon decided that even though my modest pearl set didn't outshine the shimmering diamonds, rubies and sapphires, my dress was the prettiest.

If only Greg were here. I watched the main entrance for him. I decided that I would apologize to him the minute he walked through the door. I had behaved like a selfish bitch—he had every right to be furious with me. I'd make it up to him by making love to him until dawn.

An hour went by. No Greg. I drifted on the edges of the crowd, smiling vaguely and feeling more self-conscious by the minute. Of course everyone was socializing in pairs or groups; I seemed to be the only solitary guest. *There must be someone here I know*, I thought desperately. But all the faces were unfamiliar. I did spot one blond woman I'd met during an audition. She was a model trying to make the leap to acting. What was her name? Darla or Marla or Carla. I hadn't liked her much, she was one of those annoying bimbos who was constantly striking a pose and flinging her hair around. I dismissed the idea of trying to socialize with her.

I watched the main entrance more intently, looking for that familiar tall figure. A terrible thought flitted across my mind and made me swallow hard: *Maybe Greg isn't coming. Maybe he's so angry he wants to break up with me.*

The idea shocked me to the core. I nearly ran to the ladies' room and locked myself in a stall. I balled my hands into fists, squeezing back the tears. *No. Greg is not going to break up with me. I'm overreacting again. Greg will be here soon. We'll make up and have a wonderful time.* I had to repeat this like a mantra, inhaling and exhaling deeply, before I was able to face the world again.

I fixed my hair and makeup in the ladies' lounge, chatting with other women as I primped. I felt almost normal again.

I left the lounge and was heading back to the ballroom when I heard a voice behind me say my name. *Greg.* Joy surged through my body. I turned around with a wide smile, ready to fall into his arms. I found myself staring at another face, just as familiar but completely unexpected. *David. Oh, god.*

In his formal tuxedo he looked more handsome and sophisticated than ever. He pinned me with that fierce blue stare. "How are you, Gillian?"

"Fine," I replied woodenly. "How are you?"

"Okay." He hesitated for a moment. "Gillian—"

"And how is the lovely Mrs. Wentworth?" I cut him off.

"She's not here tonight."

"What a shame. I was looking forward to meeting her," I said sarcastically.

"Gillian, please listen to me. I still think about you all the time. I want you so much, more than I've wanted any other woman. I'll do anything—"

"It's too late, David. It's been over for a long time. I'm in love with another man."

He wasn't about to give up. He gripped my arms hard. "My marriage was a big mistake. I'll get rid of Sandra—"

"David, let me go. *Now.*" I tried to pull away, but he held me firmly.

"Just listen to me, Gillian. I can offer you so much—"

"Well, this is interesting." We both turned to look at the source of the comment. *Greg*. He was standing just a few feet away, staring at us with fury in his eyes.

I yanked my arms free of David's grip. "Greg, thank god you're here."

"Looks like you've been having a good time without me. We have one little fight and you go running back to this jackass."

I stared at him in disbelief. "Are you crazy? I just happened to run into David. I didn't even want to talk to him—"

"You're dating this twerp?" David interrupted me. "I should have known. You seemed to like him a little too much that night." A vein throbbed in his temple.

Greg looked ready to explode. "She's not dating me anymore," he snarled. "She's all yours."

I felt my world crashing down and breaking into tiny pieces. People turned to gawk as I ran through the lobby with tears streaming down my face.

The taxi ride home seemed to take forever. I tossed a $20 bill at the cabbie and ran upstairs to my apartment. I tore off my dress and the pearls and threw them on the floor. I flung myself on my bed and cried for hours. It all seemed so unreal. Just a few hours ago I'd been so happy, so excited about the ball . . . and now my life was in ruins.

22

I slept uneasily for an hour or two. I woke up at dawn and lay still with my eyes squeezed shut. *My memories of last night must have been a nightmare. . . .*

I opened my eyes and faced the truth. It had really happened. My stupid fight with Greg, running into David at the ball, Greg looking at us with such contempt . . . I burst into tears again.

I finally hauled myself out of bed and showered. I made coffee but couldn't drink more than half a cup because my stomach felt so queasy.

I longed to talk to Anita, but she wasn't due back from Milan until the following week. I didn't want to talk to anyone else about this latest disaster. No one knew the true and convoluted story of my history with David and Greg.

I'd never felt so depressed, so lost. And I had to pull myself together, I was due at the studio early Monday morning to start work on *Nights of Passion.*

I glanced at my cell phone. Perhaps it wasn't really over with Greg. He'd been so angry the night before, but perhaps in the light of morning he felt differently. I hesitated and then decided to leap off the cliff. I dialed Greg's number.

Voice mail. I hung up immediately without leaving a message. *"If he wants to make up with you, he'll call,"* Miss Prudence pointed out.

"And what if David calls?" I asked.

"You know the answer to that question."

Yes, I did. If David called, I'd hang up immediately. And I wouldn't try to reach Greg again—I'd let him make the first move. And if Greg didn't call . . . I closed my eyes in agony, unable to bear the possibility of a future without him.

I cleaned my apartment to keep myself occupied. I picked up the crumpled silk ball gown from the living room floor. The hem was torn. I put it on a hanger and stuffed it into the back of my closet.

I took a long walk to clear my mind. After wandering the streets for three hours, I reluctantly returned to my apartment. As I was turning the key in my door, Natalie's door opened. She was dressed in a short pink robe. I watched her kiss a young blond man good-bye. He looked familiar. . . . I was stunned when I realized it was Justin. My gasp of surprise made them both look in my direction.

"Oh . . . hi, Gillian," said Natalie.

"Hi. I didn't realize you two were an item."

"We've been dating for a few weeks," said Justin, looking like he'd rather be someplace else.

"Well, that's great. You two are a good match."

The three of us smiled awkwardly at each other. "Well, I need to run," said Justin. "I'll call you later, sweetie." He gave Natalie another kiss and fled down the stairs.

Natalie tightened the belt on her robe. "I didn't expect this to happen, Gillian. I hope you don't mind—"

"No, really, it's fine. Justin and I broke up quite a long time ago, and of course I'm with Greg now. . . ." I faltered. "Anyway, I'm sure you and Justin are right for each other. Talk to you later."

I pushed my door open and shut it behind me. *At least those two are happy*, I thought miserably.

I decided I should eat something. I wasn't hungry at all, but I hadn't had any food in nearly twenty-four hours. I watched the local news as I heated up a can of soup. I was barely paying attention, but the sound of voices on the TV somehow comforted me. I froze when I heard the news anchor say a familiar name.

"Millionaire real-estate mogul David Wentworth was involved in an altercation last night outside a midtown hotel where a charity ball was being held. Wentworth and an unidentified man brawled on the steps of the hotel entrance. The two men were separated by a hotel security guard and Wentworth's chauffeur. No injuries were reported, and no charges were filed. Wentworth declined comment when we contacted him about the incident. Now for the weather . . ."

Oh, god. Did David fight with Greg? If so, it wasn't about me, I thought bitterly. *It was about two wounded male egos.*

The news report added another surreal layer to the memory of the worst night of my life. My appetite completely vanished. I poured the soup into a container and put it in the fridge. Then I retreated once again to my bed.

I slept most of Sunday. Every once in a while I jolted awake, convinced I'd heard my cell phone ringing. But it never rang. With every hour that passed, my hope dwindled. Greg was not going to make up with me. He didn't want me anymore.

I woke up Monday morning feeling exhausted. I drank three cups of coffee and forced myself to eat a bowl of cereal. On my way to the studio I gave myself a fierce pep talk. *Work will be the focus of your existence now. Today you're going to give the best performance of your life.*

I gazed into Steve's eyes. "It was you, it was always you. You're the one I truly love."

"And I've never stopped loving you." He bent his head and met my lips. I wrapped my arms around him. The passionate kiss seemed to go on forever.

"Cut!" yelled Harry. "That was excellent. Gillian, you're doing a terrific job. Let's take a twenty-minute break."

Steve and I wandered over to the food service table. I drank a cup of coffee and picked at a raspberry Danish.

"Harry is right, you are doing a great job," said Steve. "But you look very tired. How was the charity ball?"

I couldn't meet his eyes. "Not good. Greg and I broke up."

Steve looked shocked. "You're kidding."

"I'm afraid not. We had a big fight. . . . I can't talk about it yet. It still hurts too much."

"God, Gillian, I'm so sorry. I thought you and Greg would be together forever."

"Me, too." My voice was choked.

Steve squeezed my hand. "You know you can talk to me whenever you feel like it."

"Of course. Thanks, Steve." I wiped my wet eyes with my free hand and plastered a fake smile on my face. "It is great to be working with you. This is just the kind of distraction I need."

It was a long day at the studio. I finally got home at eight o'clock. I flopped down on the sofa and curled into a fetal position. I didn't want to eat. I didn't want to move. I didn't want to do anything.

Someone knocked on the front door. *Probably Natalie, want-*

ing to talk about Justin again. I ignored the knock, hoping she'd go away, but there was another sharp rap. I reluctantly heaved myself off the sofa and dragged myself to the door.

I opened the door to find Greg standing there. He was unshaven. There were dark circles under his bloodshot eyes, and a purple-green bruise decorated his left cheek. He looked wonderful to me.

"Gillian . . ." he whispered. I fell into his arms and sobbed. "It's okay, darling . . . it's going to be fine," he murmured as he stroked my hair.

After a long time he closed the front door and led me to the sofa. We sat down, and he crushed me in his arms again. I rested my head against his chest and closed my eyes, listening to his heartbeat. I wanted to stay like that forever.

"I'm so sorry, Gillian. I acted like such a jerk—"

"No, I was the jerk—"

"I must have been crazy—"

"You had every right to be furious with me—"

"I can't believe what I said when I saw you with David—"

"I was worse, making you feel bad about your meeting running late—"

"Can you ever forgive me—"

"No, can *you* forgive *me*—"

We looked at each other and burst out laughing. "Oh, Gillian," said Greg. "These past few days have been hell for me." He squeezed me tight again. "I was so insanely jealous when I saw you with David. And I behaved so badly—I was convinced you never wanted to see me again."

"I've been in hell, too. I was sure *you* didn't want to see *me*." I carefully traced the bruise on his cheek. "Did you and David . . ."

"Yes, I'm afraid so. We both lost it." He gave me a wry smile. "But as bad as I look, David ended up looking a lot worse."

"My poor baby." I kissed his throat. He slid his hand from my back to my breasts. His delicate touch made my nipples stiffen. I kissed his throat again and then licked and nibbled his earlobe. I could feel his heartbeat and breathing accelerate.

I helped him pull my shirt up and over my head. He unhooked my bra and buried his face between my breasts. I sighed blissfully as he ran his tongue all over my breasts, stopping only to suck gently on the nipples. I reached down to unzip the fly of his jeans, and I pulled out his rock-hard cock. I slipped my thumb into my mouth to moisten it. I ran my thumb all over the head of his cock until droplets of cum emerged.

I slid off the sofa onto the floor. I took the head of his cock into my mouth and sucked as hard as I could.

"Oh, god . . . please stop, Gillian. I'm too excited."

I released his cock and then lay on the floor and slowly pulled up my skirt. Greg wrapped his hand around his shaft and watched intently as I spread my legs and slipped my fingers under the elastic of my panties.

"My pussy is so wet. . . . I'm ready for your cock," I whispered. "I need you so much."

Greg kneeled between my legs and pulled my panties to one side. I whimpered as he slid the shaft slowly into me. I wrapped my legs around his waist and undulated. I came almost immediately, crying out as I humped his cock hard.

Greg remained still for a moment and then pumped into me hard and deep, clutching my ass, trying to possess me completely. I came again and again, the orgasms ripping through my body. Finally he shuddered deeply, moaning my name as he spurted into my pussy.

He lay on top of me, completely spent. "Am I squishing you?"

"No. It feels wonderful." I stroked his sweat-dampened curls.

He braced himself on his elbows, and his eyes locked with mine. "Gillian . . . I love you. I love you so much."

Finally . . . the words I'd wanted to hear for so long. I nearly burst into tears again. "And I love you, Greg. I never thought I could love anyone the way I love you."

His dark brown eyes filled with joy. "Will you marry me, Gillian?"

Happiness surged through me. "Of course I'll marry you."

"Thank God. I need you in my life forever." He rolled onto his side and wrapped his arms around me. I nestled against his chest with my eyes closed. The world seemed like a perfect place.

23

We set the wedding date, deciding to get married the following May at Ben's B and B in Falmouth. So much happened over the next eight months.

Greg gave me an antique wedding ring—a gorgeous square-cut diamond in a delicate setting of gold filigree. I burst into tears again when he slid it on my finger.

Chelsea Miller was pulled over for speeding by a cop in LA. The officer found an open bottle of vodka and a baggie of cocaine in her car. As the cop tried to arrest her, she took a swing at him. After she was released on bail, her publicist announced that Chelsea was going into rehab. She was dropped from Greg's TV show. The network execs agreed to move the series back to New York. Janet Bailey was hired to play Matt Blake's girlfriend. She was a tremendously talented actress who was happily married and had two children. I breathed a huge sigh of relief.

David filed for divorce from Sandra after less than a year of marriage. The breakup turned into an ugly scandal—allegations of infidelity and kinky sex on both sides. The tabloids loved it.

I wondered about Elizabeth Stone: had she helped engineer this split?

Anita started dating Neil, an architect with a sweetly geeky nature. He adored Anita, and she seemed happier with him than she'd been with any of her handsome and shallow boyfriends. Greg and I liked him a lot—and trusted him with Anita's fragile heart.

Justin was offered a new position in the Chicago office of his law firm. "He's getting a big raise," Natalie announced proudly. She and Justin became engaged and moved to Chicago, where Natalie finally opened her dating service.

The character of Serena was a big hit with soap-opera fans. My contract was renewed, and I was nominated for a daytime Emmy. Greg's show was well reviewed and attracted a large audience. The network picked up the series.

Greg and I bought a one-bedroom condo in a Central Park West high-rise. It wasn't as spacious or as luxurious as the apartment David had given me, but I was much happier living in a new place that didn't harbor memories of the turbulent past year. I was nervous about living with Greg, afraid that the petty annoyances of everyday life would damage our relationship, but sharing my existence with him felt easy and natural.

My parents adored Greg, and of course the prospect of a wedding sent Caroline into seventh heaven. "She's going to drive me nuts," I whispered desperately to my mother.

"Now, Gillian, let your little sister play. It will make her so happy to help you plan the wedding. And she'll probably be a big help."

I was surprised to discover that Mom was right. Caroline had great ideas about the floral arrangements, music, food—she even helped me find the perfect dress after I'd rejected more than two dozen wedding gowns. She and Anita patiently accompanied me to another bridal boutique—the fourth we had tried. I felt frustrated and depressed by that point. At Caroline's urging, I tried on a simple, strapless, oyster satin sheath. It fit perfectly.

"That's it," Caroline announced.

"She's absolutely right," Anita agreed. "That's the dress."

"No veil," Caroline said firmly. "Just a few flowers in your hair."

"And quiet jewelry—nothing flashy," added Anita.

"I know exactly what to wear," I said.

I bought the dress without any hesitation and took it home. Anita and Caroline offered suggestions as I tried it on again. Anita pinned my hair up into a sleek chignon while Caroline rambled about shoes. I removed a red velvet box from my dresser and took out the set of pearls Greg had given to me. I put on the choker, earrings and bracelet.

"What do you think?"

"Absolutely perfect," said Caroline. Anita enthusiastically agreed.

I looked in the full-length mirror. The pearls glowed softly against my skin. The memory of the first time I'd worn them—the disastrous night of the ball—faded into oblivion. The pearls reminded me only of Greg and of how much he loved me.

I woke up on our wedding day to find that the weather gods had smiled upon us. There wasn't even the trace of a cloud in the brilliant blue sky. Chairs had been set up in front of a rose-entwined arbor in the garden of Ben's B and B. A heavenly fragrance drifted from plumes of purple lilac and patches of lily of the valley.

The ceremony was scheduled for five P.M., so I had many hours to kill. I wasn't nervous at all, in fact, I felt perfectly relaxed, even when Anita and Caroline, my bridesmaids, fluttered around me.

Finally it was time. I calmly watched Anita and Caroline, who both looked beautiful in their pale green silk gowns, walk slowly up the path to the arbor. I followed on my father's arm, clutching my bouquet of pink roses and white lilies. And there was Greg, looking incredibly handsome and happy, waiting for me. He smiled down at me as I released my father's arm. I thought my heart would burst.

The service was brief. I stared into Greg's warm brown eyes as I repeated the simple vows that bound us forever. When he kissed me I knew I was experiencing one of the happiest moments of my life. Nothing I'd ever known before had filled me with so much joy.

Everyone had a wonderful time at the reception. Aunt Mary, my parents and Caroline, Celeste and Ryan, Anita and Neil, Steve and Oliver, Joanne and Heather, Chris and Nancy, Carl . . . all the people who meant so much to me. The food, the band, the decorations—everything was perfect. "Thank you so much for all your help," I said to Caroline, kissing her on the cheek. "You're going to have a brilliant career as a wedding planner."

The party was still going strong at midnight when Greg and I started our round of good-byes. "We're taking the early ferry to the Vineyard in the morning," we explained to our guests.

Of course Ben had put us in the old master bedroom, in which we had first made love during that memorable weekend. Greg scooped me up in his arms and carried me across the threshold, depositing me on the cherry four-poster bed. The raucous noise of the party drifted through the open windows.

Greg slowly removed the flowers and pins from my hair. "Gillian . . . I hope you won't take this the wrong way."

"What's the matter?" I was alarmed—surely nothing could ruin this perfect day.

"It's just that I feel a little weird making love here with all our relatives and friends so close by. Of course we tend to be a little noisy—"

I laughed with relief. "That's an understatement."

"So I wondered . . . have you ever had sex on the beach?"

"Oh, yes, it's delicious—my favorite cocktail. Are you going to mix me one?" I teased.

Greg swatted my behind. "You know I meant the *real* thing."

"Oh, the *real* thing. No, I've never done that . . . but as you know, I'm always ready for a new erotic adventure."

We quickly stripped off our wedding finery and slipped into shorts, T-shirts and sandals. We snuck quietly down the staircase and slipped out the back door into the cool spring night. An enormous gold full moon floated in the sky.

Greg held my hand as we followed the path to the deserted beach. We found a hollow protected by a hedge of beach roses. Greg pulled me down into the soft sand. We lay together, arms and legs entwined, gazing at the moon, listening to the waves crashing gently on the shore, feeling the warmth of each other's bodies.

"It was a wonderful day," I murmured.

"Yes . . . and now you're mine. Forever." He kissed me softly on the forehead, the lips, the hollow of my throat. He slipped his hands under my T-shirt and fondled my breasts. I slid my leg between his thighs and felt his hard cock throbbing against my skin.

I pulled off his T-shirt and covered his broad, smooth chest with kisses. I trailed my tongue down to the waistband of his shorts and then unzipped his fly and grasped his shaft. I licked every inch of his cock and tight balls until he groaned. I quickly pulled off my shorts and stood in front of him, spreading my pussy lips. He gently licked and sucked my swollen clit. I pressed his face hard against my pussy, undulating faster until the sensation became unbearable. I came with a long, low cry.

I stripped off my T-shirt and stood naked in the golden moonlight. "Lie on your back," I said.

Greg stretched out, his long shaft standing straight up. I straddled his hips and slowly slid his cock inside me. I rocked gently. “I love you, Greg,” I whispered.

“I love you, too, Gillian.”

I rubbed my clit with one finger as I rocked faster, squeezing his cock with my pussy muscles. He reached up to caress my breasts, closing his eyes in ecstasy. “I love you, I love you, I love you . . .”

I screamed as the most intense orgasm I’d ever experienced shook me to my core. I felt Greg’s cock explode inside my pussy.

I collapsed on his chest. He wrapped his arms around me, and we lay still for a few minutes, panting and gasping.

I finally slid off his cock and rolled into the soft sand next to him. He slipped his arm under my shoulders, and we stared up at the moon and stars. No words were necessary. We were already half asleep, peaceful and content, dreaming of a future with endless possibilities.

Turn the page for a tantalizing preview of
QUENCH MY THIRST
On sale now!

Sister Jenkins had a standing appointment on the third Wednesday of every month. Trevor rang her doorbell at eleven o'clock at night, and he was on time as usual. Denise never allowed him in through the front door. He was required to drive his car around to the back of the house and enter through the kitchen door. She was undoubtedly afraid her neighbors might see him and begin to ask questions. He could hear her heels clicking on the steps as she made her way down the short narrow stairwell leading to the door. She opened the door and retreated into the kitchen to allow him to enter the house. This night she was dressed in a long, white satin gown. A lone strap crossed over her left shoulder. Her right shoulder was bare. The dress dipped daringly across her large, firm bosom. Nipping in across her flat stomach, it flared out again at her hips. A thigh-high split in the right side revealed a peek at her thick thighs.

The lady spares no expense on her clothing, he thought as he started up the steps into the kitchen. He started to turn toward the bedroom in the back of the house where he usually spent his time with her, but she grabbed his hand and pulled him toward the front of the house. Puzzled, he followed her lead.

The drapes were drawn in the living room. Dozens of candles were lit along the fireplace mantel and strewn around the end and coffee tables. The strong aroma of vanilla musk filled the air. He set his bag down on the floor and looked at Denise. In the flickering light of the candles she did not look half bad, more feminine than usual.

She pointed to the grand piano in the far corner of the room. He raised his eyebrow at her quizzically. Surely she did not think he was going to make love to her on top of that piano. Women had the wildest imaginations sometimes. He would have to put this as delicately as he could. She was a very large woman, and the weight of the two of them on top of that piano could be a disaster waiting to happen.

"Honey, I am not Richard Gere, and you are not Julia Roberts. If we get on top of that piano, the legs will break like Pixy Stix," he cautioned.

"No, they won't. That's a good strong piano, and I want you to make love to me just like they did in the movie," she said sternly.

"It's up to you," Trevor replied and turned away from her. Quietly he began unbuttoning his shirt, silently praying the piano would take the strain, but there was no way in hell he was picking up her big ass and putting her on top of it.

"Wait!" Denise said, moving around to stand in front of him. She placed her hands over his to stop his progress. Pulling him over to the piano seat, she started to finish unbuttoning his shirt. She began planting wet kisses on his neck as she worked his shirt free of his pants. Diligently working on her fantasy, she unbuckled his belt and eased her hand inside his trousers.

Trevor could feel his manhood stiffening in response to her eager touch. He would give her what she was paying for. He placed his hands on her waist. The gown was satiny and slippery to his touch. He worked methodically, running his hands up and down her sides from hip to just under her armpits; delicately raking his fingertips along her skin through the flowing fabric.

Denise was growing hot and eager, her breathing quick and shallow as his lips fastened onto her neck. His breath was hot and moist in her ear as he sucked her earlobe. Pulling away from him, she feverishly pushed his trousers down off his hips. She gazed longingly at his rigid member jutting forward against the thin fabric of his silk briefs.

Trevor began nipping softly at her collarbone as he slipped the strap off her shoulder. His lips followed the line of the falling gown as it slipped lower on her bosom. The rigid tips of her large breasts held the soft fabric in place, not allowing it to fall. With each heaving breath the fabric rose and fell but stayed in place, covering her breasts. Deftly he cupped his hands under her arms and then inserted his hands in the sides of the gown and pushed it down off her breasts. Her breasts were like giant orbs of firm brown flesh. She stood naked to the waist before him. He cupped one breast in both hands and brought it to his mouth, teasing her nipple with his tongue.

Denise could feel the liquid moisture dripping between her thighs. If he touched her there, she knew she would be unable to contain the scream that was burgeoning in her throat.

Determined to give her as much of her fantasy as he could, Trevor pushed back the piano seat and moved Denise to stand in front of him at the piano. The cover was closed over the ivory keys.

She could feel the cold, rigid wood against her butt cheeks as Trevor slipped his hand into the side split of her gown. Expertly he found the wet throbbing bulb and stroked it lightly. Denise's orgasmic scream pierced his ear as her breathing became more ragged and she went limp against his chest. Continuing to stroke her clitoris, Trevor slipped out of his boxers.

Standing on tiptoe, she tried to move away from his insistent fingers, unwittingly easing herself up onto the piano-key cover. She gazed hungrily at him and reached out to touch his erect penis.

He gently removed her hand from his shaft and placed a condom in it.

"Dress me," he said huskily, latching onto her heaving breast with his mouth.

Feeling the wet juices beginning to run down her legs, Denise clumsily took the condom from his hand and unwrapped it. Fighting the weakness in her knees, she slid the condom onto the tip of his penis and began the process of unrolling it up the length of his shaft. She'd never done this before and would never have imagined how exciting it was to watch the silken skin disappear inside the latex casing, knowing full well the length of it would soon be disappearing inside her.

Trevor moved the piano seat closer to the piano and instructed Denise to raise one leg onto the stool. With the stool as leverage he was able to ease her buttocks into a seated position on the piano keys and enter her from a standing position.

Ignoring the discomfort of her position on the piano, she relished the feel of him inside her. Wrapping her free leg around his waist, she accepted the pain of the unyielding wood against her back as she pushed forward, driving him deeper inside. His hands clasped firmly onto her buttocks, holding her aloft while he rhythmically stroked in and out of her body.

He admired her strength. He knew she was uncomfortable, but she was taking every inch he had to offer. She was as strong as a bull. She was a large woman, but her skin was taut and firm. Her stomach was flat, her hips wide, and she possessed firm, round buttocks. Nothing on Denise jiggled; daily workouts made sure of this.

Feeling her orgasm again, he eased her down off the piano and led her down the hallway to the back bedroom they always used. Denise followed silently behind him. She stopped just inside the doorway and looked at him as he stood next to the bed waiting for her. His shirt was completely unbuttoned, and he was naked from the waist down except for a fresh condom, which she'd never even seen him put on. Such a handsome specimen of African-American manhood, and he was waiting for her. She smiled at the thought. *He's waiting to make love to me again.*

Trevor studied the play of emotions on her face. Denise was a walking, breathing contradiction. She wanted a man as a permanent fixture in her life, yet she couldn't yield the inevitable control over her life she assumed having one would take. If she gave herself a break, she would make a fine wife and mother. But she was too hard on herself and those around her. So she paid for the fantasy instead. He held out his hand to her. "Come on, sweetheart," he said and invited her to join him.

She smiled demurely and started toward him. Her large breasts swayed naturally with the sexy roll of her wide, rounded hips. As she started across the room, her gaze fell upon a framed picture on the opposite wall. She looked from the picture to the man who waited at her bedside, and her fantasy came alive. He was home; her man was home.

She pressed her breasts against his bare chest and laid her face on his shoulder. She breathed deeply of the essence of him and was warmed by his scent.

He nestled his face in her long, thick hair and cupped her jaw in the palm of his hand, lightly running his tongue along the outline of her ear. With his other hand he caressed her large buttocks and pressed the length of his manhood against her belly. Small asses might be cute to look at, but he liked Denise's ass. It was large, sturdy, and made a great cushion in the bed. When he pounded her deeply, her buoyant ass gave her a boost right back up against his dick. The throbbing in his dick got harder just thinking about the ride he was about to take.

Without further delay he got into the bed and pulled her onto it with him. He eased into the comfort of her soft, rounded curves. Her body enveloped his, and he rested comfortably on her double-D-cup breasts before pushing deeply inside her hidden passion.

Denise emitted a deeply satisfied sigh as she matched her movements to his. She rocked him back and forth, using the strength of her stomach muscles and buttocks to create a rolling sensation. She preferred the missionary position because it allowed her to watch her partner's expressions. She'd practiced and perfected her own special hip roll for maximum pleasure.

Trevor let her take control because that's what she paid him for, and he enjoyed the feeling of free-falling into her deep sea whenever she hit the perfect wave. He massaged one of her breasts and brought it to his lips, covering the large brown nipple with his mouth. His tongue encircled the sensitive button tip sensuously, licking and sucking alternately.

Denise's breathing quickened, and her heart beat faster. His warm, wet tongue on her nipple was creating a raging storm in her body, and she knew an explosion was near. Her legs tightened around his thighs, and she gripped his ass cheeks with her long nails.

He felt the change in her body and immediately picked up the pace. He pumped faster, longer, and deeper inside her body until her rumbling moan signaled her climax had been reached. This signaled him to release his own cum deep inside his protective sheath.

Five minutes later he was back in the living room collecting his clothes off the floor. He checked his watch. Fifteen minutes over. He would have to be more careful next time. Clients weren't allowed extra time unless they planned it in advance and paid for it. He wasn't too worried about Denise, though. Usually she didn't even keep him the full ninety minutes anyway. He dressed quickly and headed out the kitchen to the side door. His envelope was waiting on the side table as always. He stuffed it into his pocket and closed the door behind him.

Denise lay in the queen-size bed staring at the ceiling above her. The ceiling fan was still and the room eerily quiet after his departure. She stared vacantly at the white blades of the fan with the gold-accented tips, the tiny ball chain dangling beneath. She switched her focus to the E.C. Wright framed print on the far bedroom wall—the handsome black Union soldier leaning down from his horse to plant a kiss on the upturned mouth of his black wife as he prepared to journey to war. Denise had loved this picture from the moment she'd first seen it. She was deeply touched by the handsome ultramasculine soldier heading off to war, stopping for a tender moment to say good-bye to his wife.

The perfect man, the man she'd never found. The embodiment of what she wanted was only a figment of someone else's imagination. She'd often felt she was born in the wrong century. Not that she would have wanted to have been born a slave, but certainly in the after years she could have seen herself as the mistress of the plantation. Resplendent in the glorious gowns of the period with a manor-style home decorated with the finest artwork and collectibles. Yes, she could even see herself being waited on by servants. Even the idea of black servants did not disturb her dream; after all, she would be a good mistress to her help.

She shifted her position in the bed again and thought about the stunning specimen of a man who had just left her. She could picture him in the soldier's uniform sitting upright on the horse, his sword holstered and his rifle at the ready, his strong steed dancing lightly beneath him as he used the strong muscles of his thighs to control the snuffling beast. There she was beside him in her fabulous pink gown, cinched at the waist and puffing out over the crinoline underneath. Her hair would be swept up in a French chignon, with little wisps escaping, creating a subtle softness to her face. She saw it all in her mind's eye with a matte finish; painted with an artist's brush. This was what she desired most but gave up looking for many years ago.

She rolled off the bed and walked to the bedroom door. Turning back into the room, she looked longingly at the print once more. Brushing an errant tear from her cheek, she closed the door and headed down the hallway toward her bathroom.